Everybody's A Stranger

...Until they aren't

An Anthology curated by

Sindhuja Sarasram

Inkfeathers Publishing
www.inkfeathers.com

Everybody's A Stranger ...Until they aren't
Edited & Compiled by Sindhuja Sarasram
Print Edition

First Published in India in 2022
Inkfeathers Publishing, New Delhi 110095

Original Cover Illustration by Sindhuja Sarasram

ISBN 978-93-90882-54-0

www.inkfeathers.com

to everyone, who's ever been someone else's Chai or Ros;
to those dominoes

Disclaimer

The anthology 'Everybody's A Stranger…Until they aren't' is a collection of 20 Stories written by 19 authors who belong to different parts of the globe.

The anthology editor and the publisher have ensured to make the content as reader-friendly and plagiarism-free as possible. Unless otherwise indicated, all the names, characters, objects, businesses, places, events, incidents- whether physical/non-physical, real/unreal, tangible/ intangible in whatsoever description used in this book are either the product of the author's imagination or used in a fictitious manner. Any resemblance to actual persons, objects, entities, living or dead, or actual events is purely coincidental.

The stories published in this book are solely owned by their respective authors and are in no way intended to hurt anyone's religious, political, spiritual, brand, personal or fanatic beliefs and/or faith, whatsoever.

In case, any sort of plagiarism is detected in the stories within this anthology or in case of any complaints or grievances or objections, neither the anthology editor(s) nor the publisher is to be held responsible.

Made with the contributions from

P. R. M., Aanika Gajendragad, Eden Cardoz, Isha Sharma, Jigyasa Tandon, Kongkona Baishya, Pritha Samanta, Prerna Singh, Shalini Ray, Sharad Narayan, Shibani Sharma, Sindhuja Sarasram, James Bowers, Halo Golwin, Sree Yelamanchi, Suchitra Moorty, Yash Karmancherry, Yumna Usmani, Raghavi Shankara Guhan

Contents

Meet the Editor

Sindhuja Sarasram (she/her) is a regular vagabond trying to figure out the ways of the universe. She can quote complete Taylor Swift songs (but don't ever ask her to sing, please.) She hoards up antiquity, travel, soulful words, simple ideas, the concept of love, a good debate, and fur babies — everything that imprints on her soul!

After a 7-year Architecture practice, she realised her passion for nature, writing, and illustration; she hopes to amalgamate 'em, someday. Currently, she is pursuing a Master's in Landscape Architecture.

Keep up with her two Instagram personalities @motherofquirk & @albino.orange

Editor's Note

Hey Reader,

We come across so many souls every single day. With some we share a transient moment or two; with some others, an apparent permanence. But the measure of time spent in their company doesn't determine how much of an influence they have over us — oftentimes, it's the out-of-routine interaction that leaves a mark.

This book came about as a part of my journey of self-discovery, one where I set out to find how I managed to be the person I am today as opposed to the person I was a decade ago. I realised that what is within me is a collection of ideas, principles, quirks, and other things — good and bad — that I copied from my environment, that is, the souls that make up who I am, was, and will be. This concept's nothing new; we all are who we are because of those we have surrounded ourselves with.

And to speak of the strangers I met during the making of this book — they took a raw idea I had about how I wanted this book to be, and each through their interpretations of that theme, made it their own and helped me sculpt this book to be what it finally has become. And this was the only way it was meant to be.

But the irony of it is that up to a certain point, you are a product of what others determine for you. And once you reach that threshold, you partly control the reins. You get to notice, choose, and infer from your environment. When you hit that awareness, don't you feel like you need to know the pattern, the history, so that you can determine the future course? Well, that awareness struck me very recently.

I've lived in the stories that others created, and I've always wanted to tell stories but didn't know if I could. But that's the beauty of the universe – at a time when I was at my lowest, I found peace in sharing my pain and experiences through words and art — I channelize my emotions in my work, and hope that somebody can connect with it and find catharsis.

And so, I was keen to curate and tell such stories to you, dear reader. I hope these stories — some real, some crafted from imagination — inspire you to explore your own history.

Love.

Introduction

If you look at the landscape of people you've met through the entirety of your life so far, you'll realise that all of them were strangers at that moment when either of you voiced that introductory 'Hey!' or that first text. Funnily, our own parents were strangers to us, going by that definition. And why stop at listing only humans as people? Aren't your versions of Hachi and Garfield a part of that list, too?

Here, in this anthology, are a few storytellers narrating some inspired fiction and even some real-life anecdotes. And care was taken to find a spectrum of stories that were about a variety of relationships — we often find that 'two strangers meeting,' alludes to romantic relationships, especially the meet-cute and love-at-first-sight kind, while every other form of exchange between two people is grossly overlooked.

And you might ask, why are we even exploring these things? Well, here's a quick story.

Imagine you're a 15-year-old English schoolboy in the late 1950's, without godly beliefs, and are bored with the music scene of your times. But you show up anyway to your church's garden fete, and you hear another teenager making tasteful music on stage. And you start conversing and you think about collaborating. And you don't know you're influencing the course of the music industry, that even half a century later, some writer is going to narrate your story like she was there in the history-making moment and say: And that's how The Beatles was born.

While that was an example of something larger than life, every day, people we meet create differences to our thoughts, values, and perspectives; in varying proportions. They help us learn new things, reinforce some ideas we already had, or make us question everything we knew until that point where we crossed paths. While not all of those chance encounters, or the moments after, are positive or even memorable, they still affect us.

Maybe, that is the way of the universe, and the broader the variety of souls you meet, the broader is your understanding of the world, isn't it?

We exist, and then we meet a few strangers — some depart from us before getting any closer, some become our friends, some we feel something stronger for, some become icons, and some make us question ourselves, and so, forms a cycle. In the same way, in this book, some works are anecdotes about ephemeral instances; some are acknowledgements to those who shoulder our burdens; some are tales of love, bitter and sweet; some are societal touchstones; and lastly, some are anchor-points that inspire an introspection.

As a reader herself, this editor found the characters and the stories themselves as dominoes that trigger the dice of memories in her brain. And with that, she found a pattern in the stories that she received, as it is with the people we meet in life. The collection of 20 stories is thus grouped into 5 chapters, each one navigating a different thread — to list a few, through thought, empathy, sympathy, affection, love, inspiration, and finally, with self-reflection.

And now, this is the point where the stories are going to take over the narrative.

Happy reading!

PART 1

// YOU'LL FIND A RAINBOW //

And then, one fine day

1

Suhaana Safar

by P.R.M.

It was the Monday-est Friday ever!

I'd just had the longest, most gruesome day on zero sleep — sleep deprivation has different side-effects on everyone; for me, it is feeling numb from exhaustion. So, here… I wasn't hungry, wasn't sleepy, tired, or anything else really, just a giant void.

One of the most substantial benefits from a lack of sleep, in my case, is articulating my thoughts well. Like, if I'm talking about *Vada Pav*, I could talk about every detail, from the color of the garlic chutney to the crispness of the green chilli to perfectly soft potato filling. Every detail. For some random reason, not sleeping works perfectly to put my point across —always helps me during my Architecture college juries. I think it is so, because I have never been to a viva on a full night's rest — there's just always so much to do and no time to sleep for us procrastinators.

It was 6 pm, and our Urban/Rural Redevelopment elective jury finally came to a close. Usually, I would *Uber Pool* with Aarush, but today, Aarush decided to ditch me and go to party with his friends. Aarush is my *desi* friend in my master's program, and we live in the same apartment building — the ideal kind of housing for immigrant students (especially desis); with cheap and safe accommodation. The best part is that I can afford a studio apartment I don't have to share with anyone; except for having Aarush's footsteps on my ceiling every day, every footstep of his feels like a trampling elephant, so annoying! Anyway, it's cheap... So, I'm happy.

On most days, it's me by myself, because he is an extrovert, and I'm an introvert and love my alone time at home. Anyway, I couldn't uber pool on the most tiring day of my life and was rather happy to shell out for a full fare. I couldn't wait to just reach my bed and fall asleep.

Aarush texted me:

Yooooo, Sri! Party at my house tonight. Don't miss!

PS: Lotsa hot guys! So please, be there at 10! Xoxo.

I responded:

#eyeroll. Too tired man. Hitting the bed in less than an hour. Please don't break my ceiling with your *Haathi Mere Saathi* friends.

Oh my God, I need to be asleep before he gets home with his friends. Once I fall asleep, even a nuclear explosion can't wake me, especially after 2 sleepless nights. Oh god, please find me an uber and make sure there's no traffic.

I was standing outside my department and getting cancelled by uber drivers every 10 seconds. It was a gloomy cold day — it was about to worsen, and no soul on this planet was willing to drive me 8 miles! *Ugh! I'm doomed.* After getting cancelled for the seventh time, I finally got matched with a driver who didn't cancel the ride in 10 seconds. He stayed on for 5 whole minutes, and I was optimistic about this one; the only problem was that he was 30 minutes away from my location.

My phone suddenly buzzed — it was the Uber driver. *Great! Another one is going to cancel on me!* I was sure he was calling to tell me he couldn't make it, politely and decently. I picked up and

I heard the voice on the other end say, "Hullo, hey, I'm Gary, your Uber ride."

I asked, "Hi, can you hear me?"

Gary, the uber driver, responded, "Hey. Yeah, I can. I just called to let you know I'm on the way, and please don't cancel the ride — I'm stuck in a lot of traffic with bad weather and need this ride."

"Ya, sure. Okay. I can wait, see you soon."

Gary said, "Thank you, Sir. See you soon."

Since I had some time before he arrived, I decided to go to Lu Valle Commons (pronounced as *lu-vayye-commons*) to grab a bite to eat. I can't tell you how many times my parents have made fun of it and said, "So, did you eat at *loo-wale*-canteen?" — meaning 'restroom canteen.' But they have the best Mexican bowls; and are affordable for students. It's right opposite my department and such a blessing when I can't move a muscle but need food — like today. I got two bowls to go, one with fresh avocado for dinner and one without for tomorrow's lunch.

As I walked towards my department, Portola Plaza looked absolutely spectacular and charming. It was half foggy, with pockets of sunlight entering through the trees. It was mostly quiet in the evenings, and particularly on Fridays, it was the most gorgeous place to be.

I walked back to my department and sat on a bench within my *uber spot-radius* to not miss the car. The guy was coming in a silver Honda CRV. The app still showed him 30 mins away; I assumed it was probably a network issue and that the app was taking longer than usual to update his location. After another 15 minutes, it showed the exact location, and I called him — no answer. After two more unanswered calls, I finally saw the silver Honda CRV turning on the corner, and I was so relieved! I wasn't ready for another cancellation or rebooking process — I just wanted to sleep and not feel this numb exhaustion.

The driver pulled up beside me, rolled down the window and said, "Sir?? Is that you? I was expecting a young Prince. I'm delighted to find a Princess." He was grinning the whole time.

I just answered, "Yes, that's me," and gave him two thumbs-up.

When I opened the back door to get in, a lady was sitting there with a super-cute baby. She gave me a sheepish grin, and the baby was smiling with drool dripping from his mouth. I gave them both a friendly wave and hopped into the vehicle. I somehow didn't recall ordering an uber pool, but I had no energy to question it or correct my name; I only wanted to sleep. I buckled in, leaned against the window, and shut my eyes.

After sleeping for what felt like 2 hours, I was still at my university entrance, and I could read the bronze etched sign, 'University of Los Angeles, California'; I'd only been asleep for 7 minutes. The baby next to me was so excited to see me awake, he wanted all my attention. I woke up to a familiar song: *Suhaana Safar... Aur yeh Mausam haseen...* Hearing this song in an Uber with an American-Irish driver in the middle of Los Angeles was something even beyond my dreams — Yeah, he had an Irish accent; yeah, he was red-headed; yeah, he looked more like a Viking than an uber driver; but that was Gary. Somehow, it was way more annoying when he addressed me *Sir*, with an Irish accent.

I asked him, "How do you know this song? It's a really old Indian song!"

"Yes, it's sung by Mukesh — from the golden era of music!" He replied. I could see from the backseat that *Golden era of Music* was the name of the playlist he was listening to.

"Nice to see you awake, Sir. Why is your name *Sir Ja* (He said it like *Sir Ja-ck.*) Is that a common name for women in India?"

Sigh! Okay, I have to do this.

"My name is Srija — *Shreeee-jaaaa*, not *Sir-Ja*. I DO NOT have a title, and I'm NO knight; just a regular girl trying to navigate life." *That came out harsher than I intended.* I said, "Sorry, I didn't mean to yell; it's just been a really exhausting day."

"I'm so sorry, Srija — sorry, I got your name wrong. I have trouble reading the small letters on my phone lately; and I often get people's names wrong."

He continued, "I am an aspiring actor, and I came to LA like so many other people, to try and make my life-long dream of acting come true. My next audition is for a *Seer-daar-g's* role in an upcoming TV show. Do you know any *Seerdaarg's*?"

Almost chuckling, I then clarified, "You mean Sardarji? The *ji* is usually a mark of respect that a lot of Indian people use. Like for example, you would be called Gary *ji*. It's a common suffix — to show respect to elders and peers."

With excitement, Gary goes, "Wow, so beautiful! Interesting! I am learning so much from you, Sir — Oops, sorry — Srija."

"You can just call me Sri if that's easier for you."

He nodded okay and handed me a binder called Sardarji. He explained, "My audition is in two days, and like you said, I can't even pronounce Seer-daar-g correctly. Me trying to listen to Bollywood music, which my manager suggested, has clearly been useless. I could really use your help, Sri."

The whole time I was talking to Gary, the lady next to me kept smiling. I wondered why she didn't have a car seat for the baby. *Maybe she's in here for a very short ride.* The baby was edging to come to me, and as soon as I called him, he was crawling towards me. He was attracted to my glasses.

"Do you like kids?" Gary asked.

"I LOVE kids. I'm gonna have at least 4 kids with the right man."

"4 Kids? Wow! I'm good with just this little rowdy for now."

"He's your baby? I'm sorry, I had no idea this was your wife!" I turn to the woman, "What's his name?"

Gary continues proudly, "His name is Marshall — my wife is hearing and speech impaired… I didn't want to tell you I'm driving Uber rides with my family because it's not professional, and I wanted a good rating. And I am actually driving us to a pediatrician's appointment after dropping you off."

"Wow, Marshall is such a great name. I wish I knew sign language to talk to your wife. She's so beautiful," I said.

"Oh, no worries, I can just tell her that. Her name is Gabriella. Also, she can lip-read Spanish and English." He signed and told her, and Gabriella gave me a huge smile and signed something that seemed to convey gratitude. She seemed like the kind of person whose smile made you want to hug them immediately.

I was playing and cuddling with baby Marshall this whole time, and we were nowhere close to home in this traffic and thunderstorm. Since it looked like we had to stay on the road for almost an hour or more, I told Gary that I could help him learn his lines and asked him how he would like to start.

Gary spelled out his excitement, "You will? Oh my God, thank you! I would really like help in getting the pronunciation of the dialogues right and understanding the spirit of the scene."

I looked at the first dialogue in the binder and almost couldn't believe it. It started with '*Kitne Aadmi The?*'

"Sweet Mother of GOD! Are they making you act as the villain from the most iconic Bollywood movie *Sholay*, Gary?"

"I don't know — I'm not sure. I was just given this binder and asked to prepare the lines."

I explained to him that Gabbar Singh was no Sardarji. "Of course, he was called Sardar, which could be a name or just something you called your boss, but not a Sardarji," I informed Gary. I quickly read through the lines, and it was the exact scene from Sholay.

While I was looking for the scene, he signed to Gabriella, probably to relay my offer to help him, and she seemed more animated than Gary. I looked for the scene on YouTube and played it on his car Bluetooth for us to listen to.

As soon as I played it on my phone, the dialogue echoed in the car '*Kitne Aadmi the*?' (How many men were there?) It gave me goosebumps.

I paused the audio, "So, Gary, I'm going to pause the audio to help you speak every dialogue. For context, you are playing Gabbar Singh, the most iconic villain of Hindi cinema. Gabbar has asked his assistants to beat up the good guys, and he's asking his men how they failed so miserably."

"Sri, before you start, I just want to say… thank you, so much. This means the world to me!" I grinned and looked at him, his wife, and their baby.

This was the most fun I had in the longest time. Although I often had Hindi movie dialogue battles with my other desi friend Luv, this was so different. We kept rehearsing word by word and dialogue after dialogue for almost an hour, and we didn't realize the time go by.

Gary learned the entire scene like a song. He now knew most of the dialogues and could pretty much sing it in sync with the YouTube video. Gary went on to sign the entire scene to his wife; at the traffic lights, and every other interval he got, and both of us couldn't stop laughing. Gabriella signed to me and asked me if he was going crazy (the gesture I could definitely understand.) We really couldn't hold our mirth when he was working on his dialogues. Looking at us, Marshall also started giggling — like one of those screechy and unstoppable waves of amusement that babies have.

We were still a good 20 minutes from home, and so, Gary and I kept rehearsing; the Bollywood-fanatic in me continued throwing trivia at him, "…and that's why the actors and this scene are still so iconic — even after nearly 50 years of the film's release." He was really into the film's story and asked me, "Now, why does Gabbar want the hero's hands?" I found it hilarious that that's what Gary chose to focus on. I played a couple of songs from the movie; Gary and Marshall really enjoyed the beats.

We were turning the corner, almost near home — a minute away, and I was holding onto Marshall, but did not feel like letting him go. Right then, I felt Gabriella's hand on my shoulder, and she hugged me tight; and it was Gary next, giving me a fist bump from the front seat. I had tears in my eyes. I felt so homesick and really enjoyed every minute of this ride. It was hard to explain what this meant to me — I couldn't put it into words.

I got out of the car, walked towards Gary's window, and he said, "Thank you, Srija. I'm definitely going to be singing these dialogues to Marshall till he's at the age where he has an annoying father." I laughed a little and asked him, "You do know Gabbar is a villain, right? Almost like a boogeyman; so inappropriate for babies."

He stated, "I love a good villain. I'm sure Marshall will, too. Bye, Srija, have a great life!"

He drove off.

Living 8000 miles away from family, the definition of 'homesick' is something very different. You don't just miss the people — you miss the interactions, the conversations, and the smallest things that can set you off on a different tangent — one of happy memories. Hearing a familiar song, connecting with strangers about something like *Sholay*, not being able to come back home to your people — summed up my mood. Although I am super grateful for all life's opportunities, technology, and the world in the 21st century — nothing will replace the excited faces of my parents when I go home.

My phone rang; it was my dad. He started, "*Arre O Srija, exam kaisa tha re*?"

I grinned, "*Poore thees aadmi the, Sardar, aur main ek!*"

2

An Afternoon in Szczecin

by Isha Sharma

Deep breath... hold... release.

Okay, this is not working; let's try affirmations— I am a strong and confident woman.

No, no. Please, Panic, don't rise within me along with the weak coffee and eggs from the buffet breakfast at my middling but centrally located hotel. I cannot throw up in the train.

Don't worry! So, what if I don't have a phone on me? Everyone speaks English in Berlin. But all the travel bloggers said Poland is very different from Berlin. Why did I choose the unpronounceable Szczecin for a day trip? Should have stuck to Berlin! How will I know where to go without google maps? Why did I scoff at the idea of a nice physical copy of Lonely Planet, Berlin edition? Why did I think my stupid phone would be enough? Why did I decide to do a solo trip?

Calm down Tara, pull yourself together and focus on the view. Tara's thoughts were racing as rapidly as the train she was on, and she was having a hard time keeping it together. Tara held on to the cold metallic bar for support and stared unblinkingly at the swiftly altering views of grey skies, barren trees, and lush green fields.

Tara felt calmer for a moment, and she thought, *What a beautiful place... but so isolated.* And just like that, the familiar feeling returned with a vengeance— throbbing, pushing, and pulsating belligerently.

Tara felt sweat beads form within her bra and collect in her cleavage, uncomfortable and surprising, given the four degrees of chilly weather outside.

'Excuse me, are you feeling fine?' Tara was startled to see a smiling face peering at her. Tara saw that the man was looking at her with just the right amount of concern.

Tara inspected him closely and observed that he was taller than her. He was dressed in a black jacket and ripped jeans. His faded-denim backpack hung loosely from his right shoulder. She noticed that he was about the same age as her— probably in his mid-twenties as well. There was an air of calm about him that was, oddly, settling. He had freckles on his nose, where rested a reassuring set of glasses.

Tara liked men who wore glasses, they reminded her of Harry Potter and also because she had worn glasses since she was eight years old. To her, glasses were familiar and comforting— like her father reading the newspaper in the morning. She stared at the stranger, maybe a little like a goldfish, or at least that's what she thought she must have appeared to him in that moment. The panic within Tara subdued a little when she saw that he could possibly be Indian, but his voice didn't sound Indian to her; he had a pronounced British accent.

God, why am I talking to a strange man in a foreign country? What if he is a serial killer? Bloody continent has vast stretches of unmanned beautiful rolling greens, no one will find my dead body for days. What if he keeps me prisoner in a cellar? Why did I watch all those true crime documentaries on Netflix? Damn Netflix and their fine formats of storytelling!

The panic returned, and to Tara's horror, the bile in her throat rose and the next moment her breakfast was laid in a heap at the supposed serial-killer's feet. His Adidas sneakers were splattered. There was a collective 'Eww,' from their fellow passengers and genteel stepping-away from what seemed to be a five-mile radius around her. Tara thought, *Ahh, well. It's done. I might as well curl up and die soon.*

Tara ruefully wiped her mouth with the back of her hand, thinking, *So, this goes in the cringe-list that will pop up when I am trying to sleep.* She looked up at the man next to her, her eyes suddenly full of embarrassment. *Poor guy, the last thing he needed was puke on his shoes.* Tara noticed, the stranger with the Harry-Potter air had not stepped away; instead, he was offering her a crumpled tissue. He said, 'Looks like you are having a bad day.'

Tara took the tissue and thanked him. He asked her politely, while pointing to the mess on the floor of the compartment, 'Maybe we should move away from this?' Tara nodded, and both of them went to the other side of the compartment. The compartment was not very crowded; Tara observed that there were four or five other people besides the two of them. *Thank God for that. To imagine, how much more disapproval I would have had to face had there been more people!*

Tara could feel the two older women look at her with a mixture of disgust and annoyance. She tried to muster her most-apologetic expression. 'Thank you so much, for being so nice about the whole thing — I don't know what happened. I am Tara.'

He replied, 'Hi Tara, I am Zayn. And don't worry about the thing there.' He waved his hand in the general direction where Tara had committed the *thing*.

'Motion sickness can happen to anyone.' He raised his voice and again said loudly, 'anyone,' for the benefit of their fellow passengers but everyone ignored him. Zayn shrugged cheerfully and discerned, 'Eh, tough crowd.'

Tara wondered, *should I let him think that it was motion sickness or explain my predicament? Maybe it would be better to just shut my trap.* Zayn politely asked, 'So, Tara, where are you headed?'

She answered, 'I am going to Szczecin for the day. What about you?'

Zayn replied, 'Same, but following that, I will go to Warsaw. Are you planning to return to Berlin?' Tara nodded. He questioned hesitantly, 'May I ask what is troubling you?... You seem stressed.'

Tara looked up at him and in that moment, she had an overwhelming desire to hug this stranger. Before Tara could respond, Zayn suddenly observed, 'Come on, the next stop is Szczecin!' Tara hurriedly collected her backpack, and both of them got down at the tiny little station.

To Tara, the station appeared like an afterthought that was added smack in the middle of a pre-existing market. The road outside was barely twenty steps away from the platform where they stood. On the right side, there was a small station, of sorts. It had tiny kiosks for currency exchange, dubious-looking sandwiches, brightly coloured candy bars, and a few bored people.

Tara's first impression of Szczecin was that the town had an overtly languorous vibe, but it was misleading; there was an underlying edginess to the place that could strike at any moment. Tara smiled at Zayn tentatively, but before she could form any words, he asked, 'Hey, do you mind if I just use the washroom?' He pointed towards his shoes and Tara hurriedly agreed, 'Yes, of course.'

Zayn asked, 'Can I trust you to hold onto my backpack and not steal my worldly belongings?' Tara remarked, 'I am not making any promises.'

Seeing her in better spirits, Zayn spoke cheerfully, 'I will take my chances. See you right here at this bench in 5-10 minutes?' Tara assured him that she will be at the assigned spot. There was a total of two benches at the platform— one was taken by a surly looking couple, while Tara and their luggage sat on the other.

The niggling doubt gradually started building again within her. Why would a strange man she just met hand her his bag to mind? Was she going to get in trouble? She looked around to check if suspicious looking characters were hanging around but then she remembered that ordinary looking people were usually the ones to watch out for. *So, who should I look out for—ordinary people? Am I going to be on an episode of Jailed Abroad? I can feel it in my bones that this day is not going to end well...*

'I am back— sparkling clean. How do you feel about coffee?' Tara looked up and saw Zayn. He pointed to his shoes, 'See, good as new.' He noticed Tara's crumpling face and gently said, 'Tara, you can tell me what's bothering you, maybe I can help…' Tara was overwhelmed with his kindness, and he reminded her of Harry Potter more than ever.

She blurted out rapidly, 'I left my phone in the hotel room in Berlin. By the time I realised, I was already on the train. I don't have a map. I was relying only on google maps. Should I wait for the train and go back to Berlin? But then, if I do that, then I would have wasted an entire day. And I am on a very tight budget. I hate sudden change in plans. I have never done a solo trip before, but my best friend thought it would be a good idea after my…' and Tara paused, tears brimming up; her chin quivered. She didn't dare look up. Tara thought Zayn must have left by now.

Then she heard his voice, amused but still kind. 'I think you need something stronger than coffee. Come on, wrap it up.' Tara sniffled for a second. She toyed with the idea of telling Zayn to fuck-off for patronizing her, but then thought the better of it. The twosome stepped out of the station; Zayn googled and found a pub, half a kilometre away. They walked, following the directions. It was a cold and windy day, but that was expected in the month of February.

Tara found Szczecin comforting after Berlin. It was much quieter than Berlin; it had an old-world charm. Tara took in a deep breath; the chill, sharp air was refreshing. She eyed Zayn, who was walking a few steps ahead of her. She remembered all the travel blogs she had read, about what a solo female traveller needed to look out for— making friends was encouraged; it was a part of the solo-travel experience, but Tara wasn't that person. She wasn't sure how to start a conversation and Zayn had been kind of quiet since her outburst. Tara felt she had made him uncomfortable. She was lost in her cacophony of thoughts, information, and planning her opening sentence; she didn't even realise they had reached the pub. Zayn stepped inside and Tara followed.

They found a table next to a window and sat down. A sullen-looking girl reluctantly took their order for two beers. Tara was feeling discomfited, as Zayn hadn't spoken a word in some time. Once their beers arrived, Zayn took a long swig and looked at Tara. Tara also stared back at him, defiantly. Zayn paused for a second as if weighing his words, 'Look, Tara, obviously you are going through some shit, and you are trying to do something that is making you deeply uncomfortable. But the thing is, you are here, and in this moment. I think you should try and have fun. And break-ups can be tough.' Tara was annoyed beyond belief. How dare he try and tell her how to live her life?

Tara angrily said, 'Listen, you don't know me at all. Also, stop being so damn smug. Just because I had a shit moment, it doesn't give you the right to judge me.'

Zayn was taken aback. 'I am not judging you at all. I am just making an observation — take it or leave it.' Tara sat back; she wanted to retort and tell him to shut up, but she was exhausted. She said in a tired voice, 'Don't assume that I am going through a break-up.' Zayn asked, 'Aren't you?'

Tara snapped at him, 'I am, but you are making an assumption and you shouldn't be doing that. You are making snap-judgements and coming-off like a jerk.'

Zayn grinned, 'That's better, I knew you had it in you to tell me to fuck off. See, I made my second assumption about you, and I am right.'

Tara just shook her head in derision and remarked, 'Don't be such an asshole. And where did you get that accent from?'

Zayn said, 'I am from London and that's how I talk; just the way you are from India and that's the way you talk.'

Tara asked snidely, 'How long did it take you to get that accent? Two years of grad school?'

Zayn replied in a dignified manner, 'I was born in Manchester, and you are being rude.' Tara volleyed, 'Well, give some, take some.' They side-eyed each other. Tara sighed, 'You know, not that I care what you think, but you should know — it's not easy being me.'

Zayn humoured, 'You don't like letting go, do you?' Tara thought for a moment, and responded, 'I had planned this trip down to the last second and look what happened. I still fucked-up and here I am, wasting an entire day and panicking about it.'

Zayn quizzed her, 'What's the worst that can happen?'

Tara said dryly, '*Loads*! You could be a serial killer; I could get lost or get stuck in Szczecin if I miss my train back to Berlin — I won't know where I am without my phone and…'

Zayn interrupted, 'Interesting… that you hold an early violent death and losing your way at par. Delightful being you, isn't it?' Tara didn't respond and instead, leaned back in her chair and looked outside the window. Sunrays were struggling against the heavy clouds to make their appearance. Tara dreamily said, 'It's a lovely place; I can't wait to go and explore. I wish I hadn't been such an idiot and left my phone behind.'

Zayn said, 'Let's try something. I will switch off my phone, and both of us will explore Szczecin old-school — no phones, no internet to tell us what to do. Just explore the city on foot and see what happens. While you mull that over, let me add, I am not a serial killer.'

Tara shot back at him, 'But if you are one, you will be really charming and never admit that you are a serial killer, won't you?'

Zayn replied, 'Why don't we find out? And if you are feeling panicky again, please give a fair warning before hurling.' Tara just rolled her eyes at him. He impatiently gestured for the cheque; both of them paid their share.

Zayn stood up gathering his phone, jacket, and backpack. 'I am out of here. Nice meeting you!' He moved towards the door, ready to leave. Tara watched him, then she grabbed her bag and followed him hurriedly. She joined him outside the entryway; he smiled at her.

Tara asked him conversationally, 'So, where is your family from in India?'

Zayn replied, 'Not India. Karachi, Pakistan.' Tara looked at him in surprise. Zayn looked back at her and asked, 'What?'

Tara said dismissively, 'Never mind, our grandparents were probably neighbours. Also, let's not do this old-school thing, please. It'll drive me crazy!' Zayn switched off his phone and stated, 'Tara, lets live a little, we only have a day together.'

3

Second Chances

by Suchitra Moorty

(TW: Sexual abuse)

Sometimes, it is not strangers whom you fear.

It could also be someone you have known your entire life, and yet, that person could be capable of sending shivers down your spine.

'How do I stand to benefit? Will you indulge in sexual favours, in exchange of what I do for you?'

I can never forget the date, the place, the tone, the tenor and the sly smile worn on the face. I was riding pillion on his motorcycle, it was 6 PM on the 25th of March 2001. The vehicle was at the traffic sign at Nanakpura Gurudwara, Delhi. It was an alarmingly red stop light.

The man who said what he did was someone who has known me since I was two years old. He was 50 and I was 21. I was just about to start my MBA and he was a married man with two sons. He had married very late, and so, his sons were still in primary school. My parents had known this creep since the early '80s when I had just started pre-school. He lived with his widowed mother and then unmarried sister right opposite my school.

It had only been three years since my mother had moved to Delhi from her native place, Kakinada, and since, she would get very excited to see and interact with people who spoke Telugu. One thing led to another, and very soon his sister and my mother become pally. And later, their friends circle expanded vastly — there were lunches, dinners, outings, and picnics galore.

This man was a part of all these. Though I grew up in front of his eyes, he eyed me differently when I got older. He would not miss a chance to put his hands on my arms, thighs, hips, or wherever he could. Obviously, I was cringing, but I was still scared of expressing disdain publicly; because the few times I did, my mother said I was over-imagining things. She told me that some people had a tendency to touch people when they conversed and that he was in the same league. I started believing what she said and tried to put my mind at ease.

This belief of mine was shattered when my maternal cousin came to live with us. She was fairer, prettier, and more curvaceous. In those days, I was extremely lanky. One night, after everyone had retired for the day, she woke me up and told me that she wanted to confide something in me and asked me to go to the terrace with her.

'I need your counsel, Bujji,' she said.

'Ya, please go ahead... I will try my best to guide you,' I reassured here. Earlier in the day, she and I had gone to the university to submit her application. I guessed this had something to do with her studies. Her big, beautiful eyes welled up.

She said that she was very grateful to my family for hosting her and for trying our best to provide her support in her quest for high education. Yet, she wished to return to Kakinada.

At 2 AM, I was flabbergasted and thought she had lost it. I was at a loss of words. I asked her what had happened as she seemed so determined to carve a niche for herself. By now, the tap of tears had opened in full fury, and between sobs, she told me that she wasn't comfortable here.

On prodding further, I got to know that she was fearing a sexual assault if she continued staying with us. This was another bouncer. My father was the most thorough gentleman who has lived on the face of the earth and my younger brother was 8 then! I could not comprehend any of what she was saying.

At that moment, I was wide awake. She told me that the same creep groped her breast and would have continued further had his wife not walked in. My heart started pounding by then and I was sobbing along with her. I recounted all the episodes I had been man-handled by him, too. We hugged and cried; one sister to another; sharing pain, empathy, sympathy, and solidarity.

Before we went downstairs to sleep, she made me promise that I would never tell my parents of this, and I made her promise that she would pursue her education back home. Both of us kept our promises!

That same year in November, I had a full-blown experience with the scoundrel. By then, I had again tried to drive the point across to my mother that he was a pervert. Having given my cousin my word, I could only drop hints. That afternoon in November, my mother had gone with his wife to the Trade Fair. He sneaked in, leaving his incapacitated mother in bed. The children, his sons and my brother were at school. And with my father in Port Blair, I was alone.

I was all alone; even our neighbours were out-of-station.

I was in the kitchen, making myself a toast. The moment I opened the gate for him, he gave me a wily smile.

'What are you doing? Did you know I would be coming that you are cooking for me?' he said as he came into the kitchen.

'I am only putting butter on bread,' I replied.

'I am willing to eat anything you feed me. Trust me, even poison.' His grin was growing wider and scarier with each word he uttered.

He took my palm into his and put it on his chest, he asked me to feel his heartbeat. My own heart was beating 500 beats a second.

He tried to hug me. I ducked. He tried to come closer and closer. Our house had a big courtyard. I went and stood there. I saw the lady on the first floor of the house opposite ours. I called out to her. 'Aunty! Do you have light at home?'

'Yes, beta, don't you?'

'Yes, aunty. Was just asking.'

'Aunty, are you getting clean water?'

'Yes! Aren't you?'

'Aunty, does Bhaiyya live in Dubai or Muscat?'

'Suchitra, he is now in Adelaide. Is it all Ok there? Where is mom?' aunty asked me.

By then, this jerk understood that he was wasting his time here and said bye to me and left.

My brother, who was only 8 at the time, understood that something was amiss when he returned from school and kept asking me what was wrong. With his age in mind, I replied that I was having a headache.

I tried to bring up this issue with my mother, and yet again she brushed me off saying that I was over-thinking things and grumpy that she had a good time with her friend, while I stayed home tending to my brother.

I burst into tears and told her that she would never understand me. My mother is someone who has been with me through thick and thin and I am her obsession; caring and tending to me even now when I am 41; fighting my battles all the time; yet the biggest grouse I have with her is about how she could not support me in that situation.

Come 2001, when this conversation happened — it was when my mother had sent me with him to his colleague's house. That colleague's son was in the second year of his MBA at IIM Lucknow, and this pervert suggested that talking to him would help broaden my perspective and brace me for my own further studies.

When we were returning home, he told me that he would get me an admission at IIM Lucknow if I was willing to sleep with him. Otherwise, I was on my own and he on his. Everything is still so vivid in my memory; even today, after two decades.

My green top, black trouser, the red light, the car in front of us, and the empty auto rickshaw just next to his bike. The biggest regret I have is not having just jumped off his bike and having boarded the auto. Agreed, I had no money on me, but the fare could have been paid once I returned home.

I did not tell my mother anything after reaching home. The reasons being that I wanted to neither trouble myself on how callous my mother was, nor cause a further drift in our relationship. What I chose to do was play imaginary scenarios in my head where my imaginary future husband would hold this brute by the collar and smack him in front of his wife.

This time around, I confided in my brother and told him, 'I pray that his bike comes under a DTC bus, and only 1 cm pieces of his body remain!'

He kept coming to our house even after that, and there were many more such occurrences. The only saving grace was that it was all peripheral and nothing major happened. Yet, whatever did happen has scarred me for life.

I kept waiting for someone else to stand up for me and that never happened. I kept making myself and my mother miserable for preferring him over me. I have often remarked to my mother.

'If someone were to do this to Bittu, I wouldn't mind living my entire life in a dingy cell at Tihar jail by murdering the rogue!'

2012 was the year I was keen on bringing about transformational and metamorphic changes to my life. I was focussed on pursuing full-time work and finding my feet back. That time, I was a mother of a 3-year-old and was coming to realise that I had to be the change I wanted to see.

This was also the last time when this wretch tried to grope me. I gave him a resounding slap.

And I felt so liberated and free of morose. I finally rose up notches in my own self-esteem. And ever since, I have put my foot down on two things; neither would this vile person come home again, nor would my daughter ever visit his house with my mother.

God bestows us second chances to clean up mistakes of the past. The thing here is that neither my cousin nor I made any mistakes. Yet, we cleaned them up by severing ties with the person who committed the sins and have been freed of all the unwanted baggage.

4

A Friend In A Stranger

by Raghavi Shankara Guhan

I came back home tired but content, with a pleasant look plastered on my face since that encounter I had in college today. As I entered, my mother called out from the kitchen, "Arna, freshen up quickly and come for tea on the lawn."

I questioned her jovially, "What is so special today that Karuna's maa is giving so much *Karuna* to her?"

She responded in an equally jovial tone, "That is because Karuna's Maya is coming to meet her for tea!"

I was surprised and happy, "What? When did she tell you this?"

"Just a while ago she had ringed. She said she had to make up for something…" my mother trailed off.

Shaking my head in understanding, I climbed up the stairs to my room and showered. After all, I had to freshen-up quickly before that *whirlwind* arrived.

After a good 30 minutes, as I walked into the hallway, the whiff of masala tea with freshly made crisp snacks tugged at my senses. I hugged my mother from behind as she was placing the hot teapot, a set of cups, and snacks on a tray.

"See! I have been asking you for these snacks for eternity, but when do I get it!? When Maya comes home!" I lightly chided her, taking the tray from her hand. "Anyway, how many times have I told you not to strain yourself alone for these? You could have called me, and I'd have helped you!"

My mother shushed me by placing her hand over my mouth and responded, "Oh my god! I am sorry. Next time, I will send you a message when you are in college before I start preparing these. And you will skip all your classes to come to help me. Right! Now keep quiet and go place these on the tea table out there. She will be here any minute."

Just as my mother ended her sarcastic reply, the bell rang. The beloved guest— sorry, daughter — had arrived! After all, Maya was also like another child to my mother, and we had grown up together since early childhood. As my mother walked over to open the door for Maya, I called out, "Maa, I'm on the lawn — send her here. And you should join us, too; I don't want to suffer alone with her never-ending talks!"

My mother smiled and muttered to herself, "These two keep fighting, but are also inseparable… I don't know what to make of them!"

As soon as the door opened, Maya flung herself over my mom, "How are you, Aunty? It has been so long since I met you! Oh, I smell delicious *bajjis*! Oh my god— did you make them for me? Where are they?"

My mother smiled with affection; that was how Maya was, an 18-year-old teenager, but an 8-year-old child at heart, and a foodie to boot.

My mother laughed. "Karuna is on the lawn with all the food and tea. I have to run a few errands; I'll join you two after that. Until then, you both carry on!" Saying that, my mother went back into the house to wrap up some things.

After maa left, Maya came skipping towards the tea table. That was when I noticed the bag of cookies she carried. She came and seated herself on the opposite chair and exclaimed, "Tada! See what I got for my lovely Arna? I am so sorry, dear, because I couldn't wait for you during break! Are you upset with me?"

I laughed, "Maya, the mental! Why would I be upset with you for such a small thing? You and Jay just started dating a month ago! It was of course expected, and don't worry — I forgot to text you because I was caught up in thoughts on someone. And hey, I found my exam notes exactly as you left them! So don't fret, have some Chai!"

As I said all this in a flow, Maya caught onto one phrase and interrogated me teasingly, "Ooh, *caught up in thoughts on someone!?* Who is that prince charming, huh?"

"Hmm?" she nudged again as she sipped her steaming-hot masala tea. I smacked her in annoyance and replied sarcastically, "So sad that *someone* is a girl... a princess. And you know, I'm not interested, that way. So shut up, Maya — you will be surprised when you hear how I met her!"

"Okay. So, who is this? And how did you meet her? Come on. Tell me, I am very eager to listen to this story while I sip this marvellous tea made by aunty." I beamed as I recollected my day. My mother had returned, and she smiled at me, gesturing me to carry on uninterrupted.

Earlier in the day, finally, it was break time; and I had to urgently use the loo. Rushing to the one located on my floor, I was exasperated to see a long queue inside. I realised I couldn't wait until it was my turn and decided to check out the washroom in the level below mine while praying it was less crowded.

Luckily for my full bladder, it was less occupied. Turning off the tap as I finished washing my hands, I heard my phone ringing. Wiping my wet hands dry, I attended the call to hear the annoyed voice of my best friend, Maya, "Where the hell are you, Arna? And why did you take so much time to answer? I had told you to meet me outside Level 5 washroom during break, right? It's already 15 mins past, and you're still not here! Jay has been waiting from before; he won't wait any longer, so I'm leaving your notes behind the mirror. It's up to you now to find it before someone takes it! Serves you right for getting my boyfriend irritated!" spewing out that huge chunk of monologue, she cut the call without letting me explain the delay. *Wow, how did that blame fall on me?*

Smirking to myself I slid the phone back into my pocket safely as I ran up to the washroom where my important notes lay — after all, I needed those for a test in the afternoon. Finally reaching the wash counter, I stretched my hand out to inspect behind the mirror. *Peculiar place for doing this, but alright!* I let out a sigh of relief that it was still safely tucked in. Collecting it, I was suddenly thrown off guard as I heard soft, muffled weeping, and sniffing noise from below the counter. I freaked out! *Is there a ghost or something in this toilet?*

Slowly, carefully, I bent down to cautiously peer below the counter. What I saw was unexpected! A girl, another student, obviously, sat there crouched; she was constantly sniffing and sobbing into her knees which she held close to her chest in a modest fashion; she didn't even seem like she noticed another presence.

I didn't know what to do or how to respond, not even in my wildest imagination did I expect coming face-to-face with an unknown girl of my age, sobbing under a washroom counter in the corner. I just knew one thing, I wanted to help her in whichever way I could, without any thought, my palm automatically reached out to touch her hands. I didn't want to spook her.

As my warm hands contacted her cold skin, surprised, she looked up to meet my eyes. She had beautiful green orbs with streaks of brown around the corners of her iris. She looked so innocent, like a small child that had committed a mistake she now was sorry for. Locking my gaze with hers, I gave her a gentle squeeze on the hand I held, with my eyes conveying the unsaid words of reassurance and comfort.

Still a bit unsure, I spoke, "Hey. Hi, sorry if I freaked you out! I was just here to collect something of mine when I thought I heard you. I just wanted to check and... um, are you alright?"

In response, a complete reverse of what I had expected, she broke into a fit of cries and started weeping vigorously. That was when I noticed it. She clutched a wrinkled piece of paper and was further crushing it into her fist; it looked like a badly graded assignment.

Understanding, I squatted down, facing her. Softly, I related, "It's alright, dear. Struggles and stress are a part of everyone's life... Do you know I have an exam this afternoon? I am not even sure how well I'm prepared! See, I just got my notes back — and I think I might actually fail it?"

As I guessed, she titled her head up briefly, distracted from her own state of affairs and seemed curious to hear more. I continued, "Today, I slept at 4 am, as I was up all night completing an assignment due for 7 in the morning. And now, I also have a test that I've barely had time to study for!"

This caused the desired effect and she passionately responded, adding her own frustration, "But that's too late! Why did they have to schedule a test on the same day as the submission? How is that fair?" As soon as she did, she clasped her mouth shut, surprised to have sympathised with a stranger.

I shrugged, "Yes. Of course, it's not enough; and of course, it's not fair. But is it worth it? Doesn't feel like that — not now. But maybe one day, it might be." I confided, "Hence, I keep pushing myself with the belief that someday all these efforts of mine will prove fruitful!"

"Now. Would you like to talk to this stranger, friend?" I giggled mischievously as I made myself comfortable on all fours; this girl could use all the positive energy she could get today, I knew that.

She took a moment and then sighed with bitterness, "Out of all of people who walked in and out of this toilet, seeing me, then unseeing me — including my own classmates — no one bothered to talk to me, let alone sit with me. Sometimes I just feel so lonely. It feels as if I am the only person fighting, the rest are either spectators or ones here to make things worse." She took a long breath before going on, "I don't know if you realised, but just by being here and talking to me, you've made me feel loads better than I was a few moments ago. I really am grateful for that, but… Um, I'm still very confused," she said, making a puppy face. *She is so cute.*

I started giggling, "You know that being lonely is not the same as being alone, right? Now, you have me to talk to, so you are not alone anymore. So, one problem solved!" I said grinning widely, as I quirkily patted her shoulder. She let out a small chuckle. This time, there was a sparkle in her eyes. Though not exactly cheerful, I could see that my humour was easing her turmoil.

With a slightly more composed tone, she started narrating her problems, "See, half of my year is gone, and I've only gotten horrible grades so far. For the high aspirations I carry… with these grades, the universities won't even consider my application. All my lecturers this semester have been so rude and intimidating. Instead of acknowledging the effort I've put in, they are hell-bent on pointing out my flaws all the time. It just demotivates me further!"

She sighed, "My family is no better, as they are so caught up with their own issues; they won't even bother understanding my plight… Most of our discussions end in a negative note, like, 'Oh my god, what will happen to your future?' So, that again pulls me further down… And I just don't know what to do! I often feel my future is just doomed. And wow— no wonder I was having a mental breakdown when you found me!" she concluded sarcastically.

"Alright. Up you go," I held her shoulders in my palms and cajoled her to stand up. We needed a change of scenery for a change of mood and sitting on the cold floor was getting uncomfortable. *Also, people shouldn't have to catch her in her vulnerability.* I was unsure what came over me that such strong protective instincts kicked in for a stranger I had just met.

She steadied on her feet and washed her face which was lined with streaks of dried tears. After she seemed refreshed, I spelled out my thoughts, "You know. I see it like this — I cannot pick my teachers, but I can choose how to react to them. There have been occasions where I've felt so wronged and unfairly treated. But again, what can I do now? Because those moments have all passed. If I choose to, I can keep thinking about them and ruin my mood. However, I don't. Instead, you know what I do every time such things bother me?" I watched her listening attentively.

I continued, "Every such time, I remind myself those moments have passed and won't come back. But if something can make it better — that would be today, what I do today, and how I react today."

She was smiling ruefully, "How do you make yourself feel so motivated when surrounded by negativity? I just can't bring myself to do that yet!"

I gave her a soft understanding smile and replied. "How to make yourself feel motivated when you're surrounded by negativity? I don't know, I try not to absorb the negativity. People can only affect you when you let them. Once, you stop being bothered about what others think or say but do what your heart says… even without trying, you'll remain optimistic. Also, it's true that planning for the future is very essential. However, when planning, don't you think we often forget something?"

With interest, she questioned, "What is that then?" The bell rang marking the end of the break, as if in sync to also signal the end of our discussion.

As I walked out of the washroom, I turned back to look at her as I answered, "People often miss the ultimate truth that *present* is what shapes the future. In attempts to make the future better, we often forget about what we are doing in the moment." I strode back to my class, sincerely hoping I made a positive difference and not bewilderment, as I left her to reflect on things and brought her out of her low spirits, clearing the fog.

"...so that's all that happened." I concluded, in the present, to Maya and Maa.

"Do you all remember the smile I carried back home just an hour ago, maa? It was all in reflection of that one unusual, yet beautiful encounter I experienced today!" I exclaimed. My mother smiled in appreciation. "I am proud of you, darling! Such people who care for the feelings of others, let alone strangers, are rare in today's world. It just warms my heart to hear such experiences — and all the more, when my own daughter is the understanding one!"

Maya chipped in, "Of course, aunty! After all, who is her best friend?!" as she raised her imaginary collars, making us break into fits of laughter.

I dwelled on the thoughts running in my head after the meeting with that girl; I felt something. While the bewilderment was slowly getting replaced by enlightenment on the stranger's side — for me, it was some form of satisfaction.

I just had a realisation that brought on a smile; even during a conversation of that depth, we didn't ask each other's names; nor did we discuss each other's class, course, or any form of identity, really. But still, the difference we made to each other was evident; we exchanged something.

To her, perhaps, I came as a gentle breeze bringing along with me a new fragrance. The same way, I also left her with some of the sweet fragrance. To me, she came as an undiscovered scent, which I carried along as I passed, to bring a new identity to myself — that beautiful feeling of having made a difference to someone.

PART 2

// I'LL BE THERE FOR YOU //

Kindred Spirits, in hindsight

5

The Delta In The Unit

by Halo Golwin

"Do you smile all the time to hide your pain?"

"How did you...?" I stopped short; the words had come out of my mouth involuntarily as if I agreed.

"Whatever it is, I will make you smile for real and when you do — you will every single day."

No other person had exposed my true self before. It was a rare occurrence, for we were stuck in a military unit — 'the Source' — during our two years of National Service, as analysts for the army intelligence. Our main job? To scan news sources online and summarise them based on what the military required. At the behest of deadly superiors, so began my relationship with Halo.

Before Halo's arrival, all I had was Kenny. He was the embodiment of perfection, with the looks, build, and even the work competency to back up his indomitable presence in the unit. Everyone knew his future was secure, and I looked up to him with the utmost admiration. However, there was always a flicker of sadness in his eyes.

Above all the full-time National Servicemen was the all-mighty *Madam Jingles* whose reign over us was powerful and ubiquitous despite not occupying the highest position in the Source; maybe that gave her the ability to obliterate us whenever she wanted to. After all, she was the Vice-Commander and in charge of vetting our reports. Whenever I made mistakes, I recall her saying: "It's alright, I *forgive* you." Long had I been at her mercy and surpassed by Kenny in every aspect, that I was left to wonder what my place was in the unit. Despite the massive pressures I faced, I would never fail to smile every day. But then, Halo arrived.

I felt everyone's breath as they crowded around my table, anticipating the start of *the Huddle* — an endearing moment where we debated whether to report articles sent in by the previous shift on night duty.

I knew Halo was doomed when he started questioning Jingles. This rookie didn't know what he was going to reap. Halo opposed the previous shift's original decision: "In this article, India said China had kidnapped their soldiers. This should be an escalation worth reporting." In the military, you never argue with a superior.

"But is the *delta* significant? Also, we can't confirm if the *kinetics* happened since it's just an accusation; against China," Jingles responded without hesitation.

"Hmm, maybe we should keep watch for China's response first?" I suggested meekly.

"Yup, be sure to keep me in the loop if there is a *delta* on this. That's all guys; the rest should be baseline," Jingles ended smoothly.

The sheer volume of *endearing terms — delta* (for change), *kinetics* (for military action), baseline, and keeping me in the loop, etc. among many others — used by Jingles was intoxicating. But, as a staple of the modern workplace, I suppose the terminology only provides efficient and accurate communication. Also, it facilitates social bonding between colleagues in lighter moments.

"Looks like you got rejected. I was rooting for you though. I mean, just India raising the possibility that China kidnapped their soldiers...... isn't that significant? Sorry, I mean, isn't that a *significant delta*?" I spoke agitatedly. I was trying to conjure imagery while gesticulating but to no avail.

"Your hand gestures just amuse me, Golwin," Halo chuckled upon seeing me all flustered from using Jingles' lingo so unnaturally.

"If you are still so happy, I guess, Jingles hasn't driven you insane yet!" I chirped.

"*Ey*, it's okay, *bro*!" Kenny gave Halo a playful nudge. Halo just shrugged his shoulders.

This was just one of the many days when Jingles never failed to surprise us.

Another day, another scolding, it was the same old story:

"Halo! This is so badly written!" Jingles couldn't contain her amusement.

"I wrote it, ma'am. Are there any problems?" Kenny interjected.

Jingles then asked, changing the subject immediately,

"Never mind, it's just a minor mistake. I forgive you. Oh, by the way, have you tried any of my cookies yet?"

"*Ey*, it's okay. Cool, bro," Kenny comforted Halo later in vain. Halo just smiled at him blankly.

Sometime later, Halo realised there were three pimples between my eyebrows, arranged in a neat and vertical pattern. Halo looked at me with his ever-analytical eyes and remarked: "You're a unicorn, Golwin!"

"Not only because your pimples look like a horn could grow out of your head, but because you are a creature no one could imagine in real life!" Halo quipped, with a big smile on his face.

"Why?" I gasped in puzzlement.

"Remember, you said that your sister was returning from overseas? I bet, even at work you miss your teddy bears, Teddy and Polar, more than your sister does; that shows how you are living in a childish fantasy all the time!"

That was the first time they left me chuckling like the kid I truly was.

Not long after Halo's arrival, Jingles and the sergeants began hounding him with work despite his minimal training — with Jingles constantly pointing out that Halo never understood the *delta* in many articles.

Another day went by. My face sank when I saw Jingles waving to me in the distance. I regained my composure and swiftly waved back. What a coincidence that we arrived at *the Source* centre at the same time! As Jingles opened the glass door of the office, a sullen Halo greeted us.

"Halo, what are you doing here? Shouldn't you be focusing on *operations*?" Her voice was deceptively innocuous, with the slightest hint of accusation.

"I was just……" Halo stammered.

"More importantly, why did you let Sunny swap night duties with you? Sunny didn't even inform me!" Jingles interrupted.

We faced an awkward moment of silence before Jingles finally spoke: "Golwin, what do you think? If you were in Halo's shoes, what would you have done?"

"I… I… would have at least asked you what… whether you're okay with the swap!" I blurted out, unsure if I even sounded coherent.

Upon hearing my opinion, Jingles stared at Halo unflinchingly and advised him: "There are three things I cannot stand. First: people who take advantage of my kindness. Second: having the

'DO FIRST, APOLOGISE LATER' attitude. And third," she emphasised, "I HATE it when people don't FOLLOW the *Standard Operating Procedures*!"

We stood frozen, as Jingles left us to process what she lectured. What a confrontation, I mean, *kinetics* at the start of the day! Right after the scolding, Kenny entered the office, greeting me and Halo: "Hey, what's up *bros*!"

The three of us just stared at one another. A flicker of sadness passed through Kenny's eyes.

It was so entertaining every day, with Kenny constantly greeting us with his bros and Jingles mentioning the *delta* and *kinetics*. Happiness is the longing for repetition; Aah! How I wished the days would never end!

It was all fun and games until the real punchline of the joke, finally, came:

"It's just a US Navy admiral who contracted COVID-19, not the US Navy Chief of Staff. That's a *factual error*," Jingles tried her best to keep her tone light and neutral.

"Oh no! Sorry, ma'am, it must have been the way the article phrased it that led to the misinterpretation," I replied, stricken with dread. *Oh, no! If she knows Halo wrote the paragraph, he's toast!*

Almost immediately, Jingles read my mind and remarked: "Judging from the writing style, which is unbefitting of *the Source*, I assume Halo wrote this?"

The ensuing silence was damning. Then Jingles concluded: "I believe I have enough reasons to deem Halo more suitable as a collector." Her tone was decisive.

I was aghast as Jingles had single-handedly revoked Halo's privileges and robbed him of his voice in the making of vital decisions — Killing two birds with one stone! Now, all Halo was supposed to do was to simply pick up news for the analysts, like a good collector should!

I repeated to Halo everything Jingles had said. That day, something snapped in him, and things were never the same again. On the day he was demoted, he simply sat at his seat, staring blankly into space.

Noticing Halo's glum demeanour, Jingles asked politely: "Golwin, can you come over here?"

I walked towards her in numb steps. After telling me I got the dates for an article wrong again, she naively remarked about how upset Halo looked. "I gave him so many chances. He has made far more mistakes than you and Kenny."

I was dumbstruck by her erroneous assessment of Halo; because Kenny, Halo, and I were all equally guilty of making the same mistakes in our reports.

"I don't get it. I'm so nice to everyone, including Halo. Can you monitor his mental state, since you're his friend?" Jingles added. I gave a half-hearted yes and left.

"Hey *bro...*" Kenny groaned in utter exhaustion, greeting me afterwards. Neither of us could ignore the reality of it all.

Nevertheless, Halo continued opposing military authorities. His responses only became more direct and intentional. During one of our duties where Halo had been exiled to my team as a collector, our old and obtuse superior, Herry, asked Halo to transfer some photographs from a beastly old computer, an ancient machine, into a flash drive. Halo asked Herry to repeat, one of many steps he had uttered in a single breath.

Herry glared at Halo, questioning him: "Do I sound alien to you?"

"I was just asking you to repeat one step. This is a job I'm not even supposed to do," Halo put it bluntly.

That was it, Halo had invoked the fury of the all-mighty superiors again. He even got into trouble for not knowing the names of our teammates upon being assigned to my team for the first time.

I still recall Herry threatening Halo with his limited vocabulary: "You know I can check the records, right? This is not the first time you are in this team, correct?" *Check all you want! You don't even know your own teammates anyway, you old geezer.*

To make matters worse, Halo kept begging me to appeal to Jingles to reinstate him as an analyst. This wouldn't have happened if Jingles never placed me in the same team as Halo, to keep an eye on his mental faculties; If anything was worse than Jingles' antics, it might have been Halo's stubbornness.

"Fine! I will appeal to Jingles!" I replied in exasperation.

One week went by after I sent my message to Jingles. No *delta* in Jingles' impression of Halo. Also, we already had enough analysts but severely lacked collectors.

Pitying Halo's situation, Sunny, who swapped duties with Halo the last time without Jingles' permission, provided his uninformed opinion: "Dude! That's the best thing you could wish for. Just give your bare minimum here. Think about something meaningful you can do for the world instead of this nonsense."

With his lax attitude, Sunny was always a target for the superiors. Halo smiled upon hearing his advice, but he wasn't Sunny, nor did he believe he was a collector.

As if things couldn't get any worse, Ally, the embodiment of subservience, descended upon me. In response to any of Jingles' remarks, he would simply reply: "Noted, ma'am." Every day, Ally would come to me and ask: "What's the delta in this article?" I would always reply with a hint of annoyance, but Ally was seemingly oblivious to it.

One day, I noticed Halo's state of mind took a deep plunge, upon monitoring it under Jingles' command. I also monitored my disposition and realised it was dopamine-deficient, following the incident where Jingles threatened to extend Kenny's and my working hours — over my grave mistake of spelling *casualties as causalities.*

I began a grim conversation: "Don't you think life is intrinsically meaningless? Chasing something, but upon getting it, we chase something else again? I don't want to live anymore. All that is stopping me is my family. But if they are dead, then no one will care about me, and I will finally be free!"

Halo replied: "How do you live with yourself? Do you have no ambitions? I absolutely yearn to see what humanity can accomplish in the future. Why don't you ever aspire to be anything special in this unit? Humanity lives to accomplish and to see how special they can be. I did everything I could, here. But that's all I or anyone could do, right?"

"I don't want to be anything special here! Sometimes I just want to disappear! I wouldn't be any sadder if I cannot be everything I can be."

"It's not about whether you are sadder— it's about whether you can be happier."

Kenny reflected: "I do wish to be special like you, Halo, but I don't think I can. I may be something in this unit, but outside, I am nothing."

Alas, even Kenny's true emotions began to surface.

"No Kenny, I'm no more special than you are. It's just that… I aspire to be something. I will prove this by getting Jingles to reinstate me, just wait and see."

That was the first time all of us had a heart-to-heart conversation. But it was short-lived once Ally entered the picture, asking me yet again: "What's the *delta* in this article?" I rolled my eyes, averting my face so he wouldn't see.

With that, Halo confronted Jingles. A miracle or a curse came.

"Halo, we are pairing you up with Michel, so that you can teach him how to write in our lingo," Jingles instructed him. Halo wouldn't have been reinstated as an analyst if weren't for the fact that we lacked trainers to train the next batch of analysts and collectors.

Among the new generation of analysts, Halo's disciple, Michel, surpassed them all, infusing Halo's writing flair with his highly refreshing interpretations of writing. It would seem that Halo's legacy had become larger than himself.

Nevertheless, as the months passed, Kenny's, as well as my position in the unit changed for the better.

Despite Kenny's claims of not being special, he still became a highly esteemed sergeant in the unit, while I had been recognised as a seasoned analyst, highly venerated by my juniors and superiors. However, Halo's position was simply that of a senior; his juniors may respect him, but it was a different story with his superiors. In spite of it all, Halo's smile still remained.

Not much later, Halo picked up and wrote a difficult paragraph. Jingles didn't even speak to him directly about the 'glaring' mistakes he made. Instead, she called up Michel and me to discuss whether she was being biased towards Halo. I couldn't take it anymore.

That night, I wrote a horrifically long message to Jingles, *courteously advising her*, to engage directly with Halo so that she could understand his considerations in his own words. Although she responded civilly, it only confirmed my suspicions of just how petty she truly was. She said that she only asked Michel and me because she didn't want Halo to feel upset and wanted to check if his writing style matched that of the other analysts. She believed this was somehow the nicest way to treat Halo and minimise tension. Still, I knew something in me had changed, as my selflessness was unprecedented.

The status quo remained and before we knew it, it was the last day of the two long years of our National Service. Jingles thanked me and Kenny for our service to the nation. As for Halo, she wished him luck.

When it was least expected, Jingles delivered the final slap across our faces, with an innocent smile: "Oh! By the way, I will be leaving this unit today. It was so nice that we stayed together this entire time!"

I smiled in response, for the last time — simultaneously patting Halo on the back; sharing the indescribable pain we felt.

Halo responded with a wry smile: "You are not supposed to pat for that long."

With our departure… I forgive you, Jingles.

That day, Halo mused: "So, Golwin, I kept my promise to make you smile every day, didn't I?"

Yes. Halo had kept his promise — I had genuinely smiled every single day. More than ever, Halo had become a symbol rather than just a friend.

I looked up at him. As Halo smiled, it was only then that I grasped it was a smile of pain I was all too familiar with.

Was Halo's smile this entire time real? Or did he smile for me, Kenny, or himself? Who, among us here, had been living the lie the entire time? As these questions flooded my mind, I asked Halo: "Do you smile all the time to hide your pain?"

6

Finally, Home

by Eden Cardoz

I still remember that day, though, it's been a while since. I was standing outside Wilson college campus where I was looking for admission. I thought this could be the one for me, this could be home, since my elder brother was already studying here. I knew I would be fine, yet a little afraid; I didn't know anyone, and I was a shy kid.

I was as clueless and puzzled as a toddler on their first day of school could be. it's a funny expression! But that was me back then. I had this notion set in my mind that I would never find my crowd. But you see, my brother knew me — he held me and let me know that as long as he was around, I would be fine. I lived with that sense of relief and comfort, believing his presence was all I would need to survive this world which, I was told, changes everyone — 'college-life.'

While I was in my last year of schooling, I often heard my brother James speak about his college life, his classmates, and particularly about his best friends. He would tell me how quirky, fun, and lively they were; I'd wonder what was so different about them. He would be filled with excitement when he would talk about his adventurous days, and everything else pretty. It seemed that easy for him; I thought I could do it, too. Though when it was time for me to step out and see the world, it did not seem so simple.

After a lot of struggles and having finally secured admission, my very first day couldn't have gotten any worse. I had waterworks — everyone looking at me surely wondered who this weird kid was; but all I could do was sob. I was nervous to even go ahead, it seemed so hard to take a step into this new world with no familiar face. I froze there, with my brother trying to calm me down.

Across the corridor we were standing at, I saw two boys. They seemed to be the exact description of how my brother mentioned about his friends to me, but I couldn't pay enough attention, as I stood there crying, having them see me as a kid with puffy eyes and a running nose.

'These are my friends, Jordan and Sam,' James told me. I was startled, and a little embarrassed, to have these strangers see me weep. I was too nervous to even greet them back.

'Hey, you're going to be fine here. We'll be around,' these two guys reassured me. I smiled and nodded with a nervous grin on my face. Although, I did find it a little strange — the fact that people could be so accepting of you without even knowing you — that left the introvert in me, one that was always on the brink of running away when she met new people, confused... *how did they have that confidence?* I had never met people like them. I do thank the heavens that no one now remembers the day they first encountered me!

As a few days and a few weeks passed by, this college life that was described to me as fun and full of adventure, seemed like an empty road in an unknown city. A room full of unknown faces was my worst nightmare ever.

I spent most days sitting by myself or with my brother; I often stuck to him, like a leech. Being around him often, his friends began to talk to me, too, when he was busy. His friends would often let me tag along; I felt taken care of and liked by them. As I sat with them, I remembered how I happened to meet these two guys on my hysterical first day of classes.

Funny enough, across from me in the canteen, I happened to glance up to the loudest corner of the dining — annoying other people and stealing each other's food, sat Sam and Jordan. Noticing me in the room, Jordan came to the table I sat at and asked me if I would like to join them. I thought *Okay, they're people my brother knows, it can't be that terrible.* I went over to where the two of them were seated with their big group of friends.

They began conversing with me. 'Remember when you were crying in the entrance corridor like a baby!' they teased as they sat reminiscing the day we were introduced. Being silent as ever, all I did was chuckle with embarrassment. I sat there like any shy and reserved human would, scrolling through my phone to avoid any sort of dialogue.

Jordan and Sam did seem to know, literally, everyone in the room. For a kid who didn't know what an extrovert or an ambivert was, until she left school, I found these two guys really fun to be around. As I remained there wishing, and thinking, to myself that it would definitely be a different world for me if I ever turned to be like all these people — affable and quirky.

As days and months went by, these same quirky guys began to grow on me. I officially had a group of friends! What else would an introverted kid, who knew nothing about having good friends, want? It didn't bother me often that I was alone if they weren't around. I was part of a group, *I was seen!* I held on to that feeling, knowing that it was going to be okay.

You know, how unexpected conversations and unknown faces lead to the best things that ever happen to anyone? My story is something similar having met Jordan and Sam. We would often spend time together, go to the movies with everyone, run around, and generally, enjoy living in the moment. I wasn't specifically close to anyone, but I liked being around these people that made me feel accepted and loved. We would often have the same routes returning from college — travelling back home with my brother and Jordan.

Jordan is this tall, hysterical man, who is very easy to be around. When I first met him, I used to be intimidated. Our usual bus rides home were actually how I realised it was all in my head. This particular evening when James didn't go to college, it was just Jordan and I who travelled back home. As we sat in the bus, talking about different topics, Jordan paused and said, 'Tell me about yourself. I do want to know you!'

I was puzzled. *Why would someone ever want to know about me and who I am?* Being asked about who I was as a person for the first time in life, I did not stop to even wonder for a second, 'I just finished school. I like writing, listening to music, and dancing a little… And I am 16,' was what I answered. Laughing and shaking his head with mirth, he stated 'You know, you are more than your age, hobbies, and qualification, right?' Grinning with embarrassment, I paused before reflecting on my childhood, my family, my thoughts, and other stuff that's common about any average teenager's life. I opened up about the little things that made me and broke me, at the same time.

As I looked at him, his eyes seemed to be filled with compassion and concern. Taking a long breath, rubbing his palms together, Jordan looked at me. 'I want you to know that you are not alone — I'm here for you always… If you ever need anyone to talk to,' he conveyed, as he smiled. Placing his hands on my shoulders, he nodded in assurance that he meant what he said. He beamed back as I smiled. That was the first time I received that from someone.

We sat silently the rest of the ride home, listening to music, earphones plugged in. All I could think then was — *Is this how it feels like to be loved, seen, and heard?* No one had ever said those words to me before; I felt overwhelmed. It felt nice to find myself a friend; like recognising one familiar face in an unknown crowd after a long time. From that day on, just like that, we became the best of buddies. That friendship with Jordan since, happens to be one the most delightful things life has blessed me with.

James' other friend Sam happens to be one of the most hilarious and amusing people I know; often known as 'the life of OUR party,' loudest of the group, sometimes serious, but just as easy to be around, too. Well, it took a while for me to get to know the real Sam. Coincidentally, he is this other tall, crazy friend in my life.

I remember having this dull and sombre day. I waited for Sam and the others in this empty classroom we all always hung out at. Listening to music, I sat there zoned out, lost in my thoughts. I had a very jumpy reaction when someone snapped their fingers.

'What's gotten you so lost today? Something is wrong!' stated Sam, as he sat next to me. Here's the thing about Sam — he's always had this hidden ability to understand when a friend is going through something and is unable to express

With a little surprised but very confused face, I asked him, 'How do you know?'

As quirky as he was, 'I just know, I have my intuitions, I'm cool! Will you tell me now?' demanded Sam.

As I explained to him how failing a test and being yelled at home had put me in this mood, putting on a calm face, he patiently listened to me untiringly complaining about how these things left me overthinking about life. He, finally, interrupted my downward spiral and proceeded to tell me about how I needed to be positive about the little things in life and not overthink the 'tough-love' from my parents. He then hugged me and declared, 'You are brave, strong and can achieve everything you put your mind to. You got this!'

Having Sam as my friend is always like having another brother, a person who always sticks around, and is there for you when you need a friend.

I used to have this pessimistic approach towards myself, until I met Sam and Jordan. Before, I used to have a very unusual thought in my mind. I wondered why anyone with a bold and outgoing nature would want to be friends with someone who was a complete opposite of theirs.

It is an amazing feeling to have people around, the ones that do not judge me for who I am; and like me, no matter how introverted or a weirdo of a person I am. To have people, who did not think that I was overwhelming or too much to be around, was my saving grace. Eventually, I realised I had found my place in this world. They will always be there to hug me when I have a bad day and tell me the same thing they did when they first met me, 'Hey, you're going to be fine!'

It felt like there was magic in their words. I would instantly feel fine and smile as they would try to get a laugh out of me on days I was feeling down. Sam, James and Jordan played this huge role in giving me the confidence and the courage to be brave, bold, and not be scared anymore. By my second year of college, I now had the confidence to talk to people and the courage to step out and be my own person. I met a huge bunch of people just like me, who turned from strangers I would sit in a class with, into a family I would spend most of my time with. Their friendship is the warmth of knowing that it won't ever be lonely in this life again.

Life has its beautiful and unexpected ways of showing you that it is okay to feel disoriented on an unknown road in an unknown city because someday soon, those empty roads won't feel lost —

you will find your way, you will learn to hold on, and you will know yourself, soon.

All my life, I had this dim view that I was a difficult person, despicable to be around — until two years later, when I had a mind-awakening, eye-opening realisation that for 17 years I had a friend, who lived with me, loved me, and was there for me through my rollercoaster years of experiencing life, my brother James. And it was he who showed me the world, this college life and coincidentally led me to having beautiful friends like Jordan and Sam and setting me on my own path.

That timid girl who did not know how to be around other people nor herself before, today, writes to you about how it all comes down to these unexpected conversations and unknown people, who go from knowing nothing about you, to leaving footprints on your life and transforming your entire world a 360 degree.

We celebrate the smallest achievements each one does, we come running first when something is wrong, and we all just exist to be there for each other today. Changes do happen in life, they may bring you the best, they may bring you the worst, too; the 'yin-yang.' I was blessed to experience a good change to life.

This is my journey from being lost to never again being alone — a road that has led me, finally, home.

7

The Six Sparks

by Shibani Sharma

How true, this is. Everyone wishes for that one spark to come alive from within themselves, but how does it get there? Do we bring it out ourselves or is there another person behind this spark? And can there be more than one person igniting us?

Well, in my case, they are my constants — a whole band of friends who have stuck with one another through thick and thin.

The scene of the first lecture on the first day of my TYBA (Third year in sociology) is still vividly imprinted in my head. It was a really bright day and a few rays of the summer sun from the big windows created streaks on the mosaic of our classroom floor. The professor teaching this class had stepped in and no sooner did the bell ring indicating the start of the lecture. She seemed to like throwing the impression of 'no tolerance for nonsense.'

'Hey, we have a late-comer!' Sloane whispered to me.

In a theatrical way, there strode right into the doorway a very confident and attractive girl. She was so engrossed with her own entrance that she missed the red-faced lecturer's glare on her back. Simply seating herself behind me, she removed her long book and a pen, and looked ahead grinning without cause.

'A very good morning to you, ma'am!' Shanaya greeted aloud as she finally noticed the older woman staring at her.

After a few seconds, the professor turned to the blackboard to calm herself. Meanwhile, Shanaya in her own friendly way went on to introduce herself in whispered tones to her neighbour and a couple of us peers who were sitting around her.

'Did you take permission to come inside the class? You were late and entered the classroom after the bell rang,' turning around to face us once more, our lecturer spoke as loud as her really soft voice could carry.

'Sure,' stating this, Shanaya again walked in slow motion and stood outside the classroom.

'May I come in, ma'am?' Holding her right arm out, like how we did as kids in school, Shanaya asked for permission with a charismatic smile.

My first impression of Shanaya was that of a clean-hearted girl. And she was so jovial on the first day that, looking at her, everyone felt refreshed and positive; with the way she presented herself, all the irritation drained off from our lecturer's face.

'Yes, come in and make sure tardiness doesn't become a habit going forward — I do not appreciate late-comers, alright!' Our lecturer stated in a strict tone; thinking that she made a point, she smirked as she lifted the open book in front of her face.

'Hi, I am Siya! And where have you been, friend?' I turned around and spoke in a friendly way.

'It is so nice to meet you, Siya,' Shanaya responded.

'Welcome to the class!' Sloane greeted, turning back as well and smiling at Shanaya.

A few students giggled, a few threw sly-looks at Shanaya, but in the end, most of them had a big smile on their faces because of this one girl. However, for me, she was no more a stranger from that moment— I looked up to her for her free spirit.

Sloane and I introduced Shanaya to a few of our peers, Aaditi, Maayra and Avanti. And we all started sitting in a group whilst attending lectures. After a couple of days, we had another addition. Our row in the class was definitely less-occupied, hence, any new person entering the room always ended up sitting around us.

This time, the new girl was petite-framed and a little shy. She was sweet and so, our group was taken with her. But it took me some time, to see Samaira's real self and connect with her.

One day, we had a surprise test by the same 'no tolerance for nonsense' professor. Because Samaira was a few days late to classes, she did not have all the notes for this chapter on which the test was being conducted. She did try informing our lecturer of the same, but as I mentioned earlier, her policy was without mercy, so she refused to budge from her decision and made poor Samaira take the test anyway.

And, to top of it all, she also announced in the class that if she got more than half of the class to do well in this one little test, she would take the same into consideration as an add-on average for our viva or projects towards the end of the semester — that would boost our final score.

We students were all in the habit of occupying the same places, so I was always on the third desk from the front; that day, Samaira sat right behind me. When the test commenced, I started putting onto paper whatever I could recollect. Looking at me go, Samaira nervously poked me on the back with her forefinger.

'Can you please show me your first answer? I can peep into your answer sheets if you turn it a little to your left,' she whispered.

'Hmm, okay,' That was all I could respond. I turned a little sideways, to reveal my desk to this new friend I made a few days back.

Anyone who knew me, knew that I did not cheat — although, that didn't refrain me from helping my friends. I've always had a tendency to be there for my friends, and here I realised I'd bonded yet again, when until the last question and umpteenth time that I got poked, I tried my best to be helpful to Samaira. And in her own way, unaware, she became that friend who always brought a silly smile to my face.

The days passed and there came the infamous Mumbai monsoons. It was the year 2012, and our lectures were cancelled due to the waterlogging around our campus.

A handful of us waited for our class to begin when the announcement came, that all the students were instructed to leave for home right then and the college was to remain closed for the rest of the day.

Our group was the only one left in the classroom when — boom — in a blaring volume, a song started playing from a phone resting on the front desk, *'Pal pal na maane tinku jeeya, arey, tinku jeeya...'*

Mouth agape, I saw this amazing energy on the teachers' podium. Swaying to the music was the star Avanti in the middle, flanked by Shanaya and Samaira on either side of her. Avanti let her hair down, twirling to the beats of the laughable song. Not concerned for our reactions, she seemed to dance to entertain herself.

Caught in the frenzy, Sloane, Aaditi and I started hooting and cheering for them to go on and dance, whilst Maayra watched us, trying to contain her giggles.

'What are we girls doing? What if we get caught? Should we even be here, after being told to go home?' Maayra puzzled the crowd with an innocent tone, while taking a video of us on her mobile phone.

'Hey, yes! But before we depart, please do share the video to our WhatsApp group, Maayra!' I said playfully.

Avanti had touched me too when I saw how carefree and her own self she was while dancing. From that day on, whenever I was around Avanti my heart tugged and spoke to me to live life for myself and be free of all the things that weighed on my teenage mind. And this way, from Avanti I learned to stress less about the things that I couldn't control but live with contentment for all the things that were within my control!

It was that time of the year when our college fest was upon us. Everyone was excited, and the corridors were always vibrating energetically with murmurs, gasps and coos in the weeks leading up to it.

'We have to participate in something — we have to get our group out there! What do you say, girls?' Aaditi asked us all, with hopeful eyes.

'Well, I can think of something that we all can do together,' Shanaya quickly responded.

'What is it? Tell us,' Avanti enquired, nudging Shanaya.

'We can participate in the modelling event, yeah! What do you pretty girls think?' Shanaya stated beaming at the rest of us.

'Hey, I like this idea. I know people who are organizing the event. Shanaya, you are brilliant!' Aaditi responded, in full agreement.

'Hey! We guys are not sure, though,' Samaira, Maayra, Avanti and I spoke together in unison.

'Why? We all are beautiful, and at least, we all can give it a try,' Shanaya coaxed.

'You have modelled before, and Aaditi too; she is one of the tallest students in our batch!' Maayra laid out the facts.

'Yes, but who knows, we could get selected... And how will we know if we don't even try? Please, guys!' Aaditi encouraged.

'Ok, we'll try!' I spoke for us, after getting nods of approval from the others.

'Great! After this lecture, we are to go down to the 2nd floor. I just got the information,' Aaditi stated, excitedly waving her phone screen in front of us.

Once our final lecture ended and twenty whole minutes later, we managed to reach the allotted classroom where the auditions were happening. But we were already tired of listening to Avanti and Shanaya bicker with each other.

'Okay, stop it you, two! We are here now, so let us focus on the audition,' Aaditi tried putting a stop to an already brewing argument.

'Well, we would have gotten here sooner if we didn't stop at every step to talk to people!' Avanti complained with an irritable tone.

'It is not my fault that everyone knows me and wants to greet me or talk to me for a few seconds!' Shanaya defended herself.

'Sure, a few seconds are bearable; but having to stop and talk to almost everyone — for minutes, that's just weird, especially, when we all have something to do. It was your idea...' Avanti retorted, with a little more firmness than she wanted.

'Yes, my idea — to which you all agreed,' Shanaya clarified.

'Okay, can we keep our opinions to ourselves until after we audition? Please! This is the first thing that we are doing as a group... Come on, girls. Hug it out, you two!' Aaditi declared hence, helping in easing all of us once again.

I picked up on Aaditi's perceptive nature; she was the empathetic girl, and she motivated everyone. She never let any of us feel low for too long. She was easy to talk to and made us comfortable by encouraging us with her sensibility.

Unsurprisingly, Aaditi became the problem-solver of our group. The rest of the gang went to her in case of any problems; she would happily hear us out and advise.

Time flies, and so it did for our college life... That final year was almost coming to a close when there was another announcement made in the class: Any student whose attendance for the whole term was below 75% was not going be allowed to sit for prelims; and that was surely going to be an obstacle for them to give their board exams that year.

Maayra was told by one of our teachers that she was right on the threshold. She was asked to inform her parents, who had to see to and give their word that she would keep attending all the classes until prelims.

'What am I going to do? I have less than 75% — guys, think. Please!' Shanaya squeaked in a nervous tone.

'Hmm... Your mother or father cannot come and assure the professors that you will not miss out on any days going further?' Maayra enquired.

'No. At least, you are on the dot with 75%. My attendance is much lower; and my parents are pretty strict where attendance is concerned. What am I going to do?!' Shanaya squeaked, a little more panicked.

'Okay. My mother cannot come because she is travelling, so instead, my elder brother has agreed to come meet the teachers. You have an elder brother, too, if I remember correctly. Can't he come, speak for you?' Maayra suggested and smiled supportively.

'Hey, that is a brilliant idea! I will try getting my brother to do that. Thank you, Maayra!' Shanaya exclaimed with relief.

And that day, Maayra, the wise one became a big influence on me! She had guided and found a solution for a friend to get out of a dire situation.

But my first spark of that year was none other than Sloane.

We had studied together in our second year. But back then, we each had a different gang of friends. That term, we both hadn't done quite well in Psychology, and that forced a year's break on us. When I entered the classroom on the first day of final year, her face was the only one known to me; and in turn, I was the only one Sloane recognised, too.

She glanced at me with a broad smile and called out, with a big wave of her hand to come sit with her. We both knew what we went through, and never felt the need to talk about it. With the mutual and unspoken understanding — knowing that we had company, in each other— the term ahead got so much easier to deal with. Sloane always had a selfless smile on her face; and she blended in with the rest, in her own way.

From afar, we each had different characteristics. People merely stared at us when they spotted me and my band of friends. Eventually, we stopped worrying about what others thought of us. We fit in, anyway! We knew that year was going to turn out to be epic for all of us, and we made it so!

Having so many unforgettable memories made together — within the span of that one year — we still can't believe that it is 2021 and we are all still connected; we have discussed about everything under the sun. I have read this thing that, between the age of 16 - 26 years, we meet a lot of temporary people. Yes, situations brought us together, yet we chose to stick around. And so, I can vouch for all my sparks and myself that we have been constants for one another since. And shall remain that way.

The world that we live in is magnanimous and a lot of us are not even aware of it. We have grown up hearing and believing that when gestures that are kind, cheesy, or lovable are shown to us from another person, then we automatically find in them a true friend, companion, or a well-wisher.

And in the quest to find such a person, we tend to neglect and do not pause to consider the little things that happen in the day-to-day monotonous routines that we have carved our lives into. And seldom do we pay heed to the people we meet, who in the end, become dear to us than just be mere strangers from that first crossing of paths.

It is a big world out there, and these are the people who are no more strangers to me. I love and cherish every bit that got us all close. Even if I came across one of them in a sea of people, I'm sure that I can isolate them from the crowd— and them, me. We are our own people and I wish for you to find yours, too! And, if you already have that kind of a bond where you found your own person — then, please — cherish them, the bond, and be there for each other!

8

Underneath The False Bravado

by Aanika

'Bye, sweethearts! Have fun.'

'Bye, Mrs. Collymore,' we replied in unison as we got on the bus. My first day of school. Literally. At 15 years old, I had never been to school before. No, I was not a kindergartener; I had been home-schooled all this while— Well, orphan-schooled. My father... well, he left me and my mother when I was just a baby; before I even got to recognize him. However, my mother stayed with me until I was four when she decided to send me to an orphanage.

She sent me away because she had fallen ill— until I turned older, I didn't even know what the disease caused, except for leaving me motherless. She had to be admitted to the hospital every two weeks and she thought she couldn't handle me on her own. She could have instead sent me to grandma's house, but it wasn't meant to be. So, she left me with strangers and never visited me since. Maybe the disease was serious, still, I would've liked to see her once, at least. Though, now I'm happy I have Pearl and Collymore.

Anyway, I was both eager and nervous to go to school. My friend Pearl, on the other hand, was freaking out. 'Isn't it so exciting? We're going to school!' she squealed. Unfortunately for her, she was an orphan since her birth. Collymore is her aunt, though she might look like her grandmother. Don't get me wrong, I love dear old Colly; she's the reason I live today.

After what felt like forever on the bus, we finally reached the school. It looked grand— and why wouldn't it be, in the context of charity people pay to the orphanage nowadays? Students bustled around, smiling at each other in greeting.

***

'Your class, Pearl and Valerie, is to the left of the stairs— on the first floor. Have a great first day!' said the clerk at the principal's office. The instruction seemed simple enough; I thought we wouldn't need anybody's help. I led the way, holding Pearl's hand in mine, and avoided eye contact with anyone looking our way. I was an introvert, you see.

Luck wasn't on our side today, though. *Which, out of the 4 four staircases, was the woman talking about?* We managed to mess up in the first hour of the day by getting lost. Believe me, the campus was *huge*. Pearl, being the extrovert— the life of the party, talkative— walked up to a girl and asked her in her sweet voice, 'Hey, excuse me. We're new here, as you can probably guess... Can you point us to the B-14 class?'

The girl looked us up and down and scoffed. 'Aren't you the orphans I always see while crossing that orphanage? God, you guys are so annoying. Don't make as much noise as you used to in your sweet home— this is school!' she chewed out. That was when I recognized her.

She was the same bratty 10-year-old who brought her mom to scold us when we accidentally threw a ball on her head. That was 5 years ago, and I almost forgot the incident, but not quite. Oh yes, it was the same grating voice, and eyes— etched in my memory. She now wore a beanie over her head, letting her long ash-blonde hair cascade down her back. Her sapphire blue irises, under the long bangs, pierced right through me. She had a black full-sleeved tee, and black jeans on.

Another girl approached her just then. 'Bee, what are you doing? Come on,' she gestured. But Bee's eyes stayed on us. On me. It was like she hated me with a passion.

'Let's go, Cass,' she said after she was done staring at me. She was already giving me bad vibes.

'Wait! They didn't tell us where the class is,' Pearl sighed.

'Let's just follow them... maybe our class is around there,' I suggested.

We saw the two girls enter a room. Which was, unfortunately, B-14. We followed and sat at the front, much to Pearl's protests— because the first period was history. What did she expect? — I love the subject!

***

It was already lunch break. There wasn't much of a difference between learning here and being taught at home, to be honest, but I enjoyed school; I'm glad Colly got us in.

Pearl and I walked to the nearest table in the cafeteria, with the trays in our hands. Luckily, both of us were in the same room for every subject.

'Today was fun, wasn't it?' I asked, sitting down in front of my friend.

'Sure was,' she raised her eyebrows sarcastically.

'The day isn't over. We have P.E today!' she winked at me. Ugh. The only thing I hate is sports or anything to do with moving, really.

'Move,' we heard someone say. I looked up to see the Queen Bee with her sidekick Casserole or something. 'Uh… what?' I questioned.

'I said move. This is our seat,' she demanded.

'We can share,' Pearl said, fear evident in her tone. I wouldn't blame the poor kid— It was her first day as well. I've watched movies that had scenes like this.

'We don't share. Move!' Bee scoffed. I didn't even know if that was her real name.

'You heard Beatrix,' her little sidekick, Cassette, said as if she read my mind. So, the name was Beatrix. I stood up and clutched my fists. I didn't know why, but I felt heroic.

'We came here first,' I spewed.

'I don't care. This is our seat,' she repeated. Suddenly, I felt a warm and gooey liquid running down my forehead. I wiped some off my face and looked at it only to find out it was a chocolate milkshake. I gasped, catching everyone's attention. Great. The first day, and I was already embarrassing myself.

I turned to Cassino, who was laughing her head off. Was her name Cassino? Everyone in the cafeteria started laughing, while the two miscreants high-fived each other. In reflex, I pushed Cassino.

'How dare you hit Cassandra!' Beatrix bleated. And slapped me. Could the day have gotten any more dramatic? And it was only the afternoon, yet.

I felt enormous rage and reacted with my arm swinging towards her face. 'You-'

Cassandra held my hand before I could touch Beatrix.

'Not her. Don't you touch *her*,' she gritted her teeth. Weird. I let it go because she looked intimidating. And I didn't want the rest of the cafeteria to watch us as if they were glued to a movie.

I walked away, not failing to hear Beatrix whisper a thanks to her sidekick. It wasn't my business though, that's why I didn't turn around.

***

The month passed by, faster than I thought it would. I was still on bad terms with Beatrix and Cassandra. We were like nemesis, for reasons I didn't understand. As for the rest of it, I was getting along pretty well with some people, and doing well in my studies, too. Pearl was still my best friend, of course.

Before the first period, I was walking to my locker when someone bumped into me, making my books fall. It was Ms. Queen Bee. *How surprising.* 'Oops, sorry!' she said, in her best trying-to-be-innocent voice and left me picking up the fallen books. This became a pattern; it was, soon, a daily routine. She wouldn't go a day without annoying me, that brat.

I entered the classroom, with a sigh of relief seeing the teacher hadn't arrived yet. I was late for two days straight because of Beatrix and Cassandra. Pearl made weird faces at me, as I was reaching for my seat. I chuckled loudly and was about to sit—before someone cleared their throat. I slowly turned my head around, to see the teacher folding her arms across her chest.

'Tardiness three days in a row, Valerie? Detention.'

I glared at the laughing duo I called my enemies. When the teacher looked at them, they shrugged innocently.

'Aww, don't sulk, sweetie,' Beatrix cooed to me after the hour was up.

'Go away,' I said. I got a laugh in response.

That was it. I couldn't bear to get scolded by Colly for misbehaviour. She was sweet most of the time, but you didn't want to see her when she was mad. Something snapped within, and I smacked Beatrix hard across the face. This was the first time I laid my hand on her. Everyone, including Beatrix, gasped. She held her cheek and ran out of the room.

I felt a sharp jab on my arm.

'I told you not to touch her, you jerk!' Cassandra growled and ran after her friend. I was puzzled. *Why does Beatrix have to be so dramatic? And why is Cassandra so protective of her?*

A girl walked up to me and whispered, 'You shouldn't have done that.'

She walked away before I could ask her why. *Never mind, it's probably because she's the popular kid. And bully.*

I was near my locker again, this time, after school. I caught a glimpse of Beatrix and Cassandra; both were avoiding eye contact with everyone. 'Hey, bestie,' the voice startled me. It was only Pearl. 'I heard you had a tussle with Beatrix,' she said. Right, Pearl wasn't there when that happened. She had basketball practice early in the morning. She's athletic and all.

'I don't know why people are making such a big deal out of it,' I replied. 'Bee, herself, is sulking— *Who knew?!*'

Another boy I hadn't met before, approached me.

'You're the one who slapped Beatrix, aren't you? You shouldn't have. You are gonna regret it soon.' He said and walked away.

'Look,' I pointed out, exasperated. 'At least ten people have said the same thing to me, today. And others have given me strange looks.'

'Hmm, why don't you spy on Beatrix and get to know yourself?' Pearl suggested.

I widened my eyes at her. 'Are you crazy?'

'You're the one trying to figure her out,' she shrugged. She was right, I was curious.

'Even though my mind keeps telling me it's because she's popular, I feel like it's something else. But I've never spied before.

I don't know how it'll go.' I took a deep breath. 'Well then, wish me luck.'

'You go girl!' she clicked her tongue at me.

I saw Beatrix standing near her locker, without Cassandra, so I walked close to her.

It was hard to keep up, as I followed her outside the school. Soon, she took a turn and reached an abandoned-looking street. Now I was *really* intrigued. She then went toward an old building that had dried creepers hanging on the walls. I stood at the edge of the fence when she walked inside.

'Hey honey, how was school today?' A woman I recognized to be her mother asked, as she tenderly tucked a few locks of hair behind Beatrix's ear.

'T'was good,' she replied but flinched at her mother's gesture.

'Beatrix, why is your cheek red? Did someone hurt you again? The doctor asked you to stay away—'

'It's okay, I'm fine. It really doesn't hurt.'

'Don't lie, honey! The last time, you said that you couldn't go to school for a week because of your—'

'I said I'm fine, mom,' Beatrix whined, interrupting her mother again. I stepped a little closer to the house, without realising there was a dry leaf below my leg. It made a loud crack, which drew the attention of the two. I dashed, quickly, before they could turn around. I don't think I've ever run as fast as that.

I was pretty embarrassed to go to school the next day, but Colly wouldn't let me bunk. I noticed Beatrix ignoring me and I was fine with it, as long as it didn't make things more awkward.

But that didn't last long. We bumped into each other in the washroom.

'I-I'm sorry,' she said.

'No, I'm sorry, you know, for yesterday. I shouldn't have struck you,' I said back. She shook her head. 'It's fine, I'm fine.'

'So…' I started.

'So…' she repeated.

'Uh, why do people keep saying I shouldn't have... to you?' I asked. She was, clearly, the wrong person to ask the question to—but it came out of my mouth, anyway. She looked taken aback, at first. 'I have these— *lesions?* On my skin,' she paused. 'I… I don't even know how to pronounce the disease. *Basal cell car—* something.'

Whoa. That was all of a sudden.

'*Basal cell carcinoma?*' I asked her.

'Yes. That.'

'My mother had it, too. I couldn't help her at that time because I was young. Then she left me. I don't even know if she's still alive. I never heard from her, or of her… after she left.' I wasn't sure why I was telling her this; also, I was feeling regretful about hating Beatrix all this while.

'It isn't your fault... You didn't know,' she said, looking at me. 'And I'm sorry about your mom.'

'Yeah, no…' I gulped, 'I'm so sorry. Like *really* sorry. I mean, I wouldn't have— if I'd known. Well, shouldn't hurt anyone in the first place…'

'I know. I shouldn't have annoyed you, too. I don't know why I did that.' She stated.

She took a deep breath and continued, 'I don't know… I wanted to feel good about myself for once, I guess. The fact that you don't have your parents around made me feel like I could look down on you, and that was completely wrong of me.' Beatrix swallowed, 'I'm sorry.'

'You're fine now?' I asked, to which she nodded.

'Yup. Fine. You needn't worry.'

We stood in uncomfortable silence, for a few minutes, before she cleared her throat. 'So, were you the one snooping on me yesterday?'

Great. Just when I thought I wouldn't be more embarrassed. 'About that…' I trailed off, which made her chuckle. 'Sorry,' I said sheepishly.

'It's no big deal.' She hesitated for some time; I think she wanted to share something.

'What's wrong?' I asked. She removed her beanie. Then, her hair. Wig. Her forehead and scalp had small red spots all over— which, I figured, were lesions.

'You're beautiful,' I whispered. Her cheeks turned red.

'I think I'm ready to show 'em who I truly am.' She took a deep breath and fisted the wig in her palm. I held out my arm to her. We walked out hand in hand, with her smiling proudly— at the people gaping at her head.

PART 3

// ALL TOO WELL //

Of love, or something like it

9

The Scent of Certain Old Books

by Shalini Ray

These days I often wake up screaming. The moments leading up to the scream and the hazy dream scenarios that my mind makes up are not terrifying at all.

No, these moments of anger, of rage, lead up to helplessness. It builds up, further and further until I cannot contain it anymore, and then I'm usually woken up by my flatmate Jaya.

I don't really like my flatmate Jaya. It's nothing in particular; she's just everything I would not be. The beige, pink, and creamy, lacy clothes, the ruffle collared shirts; the accent which God knows came from where, since both her parents were from Kolkata — she lived there all her life until now; the shrill way she would call out my name; I could go on.

I, on the other hand, was a heap of nothing — which is not anything better — but at least, a heap of nothing took no shape or form, and did not disturb anyone's peace; until now. The night terrors were truly uncalled for; because now, suddenly, I was taking up space.

I always had vivid dreams. When I was a child, my mother would read various books to me. Later, I would dream about the scenarios in the stories; my imagination ran wild — nothing ever truly ended in the pages of a book even after the chapter had ended. After she passed away and I read those books myself, I found out that she often twisted the endings; made them brighter, happier. Maybe she thought that way, they were better suited for a child's imagination.

There was one book I liked in particular. It was called *Irzaya*. The story was about Death counselling a young child before he passes away. My mother had replaced Death with a fairy godmother, and the dying kid with a sleeping one instead. I liked the original story better for obvious reasons. It made more sense as a story to a child who had suddenly lost a person and could not find them no matter how hard they tried. As the dying child reaches his final hours, Death tells the child to not be afraid because it would feel like falling asleep, tumbling down a staircase suddenly till you faded into nothingness.

My mother understood that the story could be used either way. Now at thirty-two, I had a corporate job — it was secure, tedious, and drained every morsel of energy I had in my life. Though, I don't think I had much energy to begin with. I lived in an overcrowded city, in a two-bedroom flat with the aforementioned flatmate and her boyfriend. He wasn't our flatmate per say, but he might as well have been since he was always there.

I took the public train to work, it was a forty-minute commute to and fro. On the weekends, I visited my father. He lived in Pune, a two-hour ride away. His second wife hated me, and at times, I felt like he wasn't too fond of me either. But he was old and was going into the early stages of dementia. So, despite myself, I visited him.

He asked me one day if I planned on being alone forever over a glass of neat scotch. I said yes. He had always been an alcoholic. He preferred his alcohol neat. I pretended to like it neat too, in front of him. That night when I slept, I dreamt that I was desperately yelling for my father on an overcrowded platform as people swarmed into the trains. I screamed at the top of my voice, but he could not hear me. Jaya came and woke me up.

I did not mind being alone, I could shut off my mind when I was alone. At times, I was afraid that I felt nothing. Worse than nothing, I felt... empty. As if someone had taken something out of me and replaced it with dog shit. It used to get me so nervous that I tried *Xanax* a few times. But that just made me feel numb.

Jaya said she could get us Ecstasy from her boyfriend. He was a pothead and casually dabbled in other drugs for what he called *spiritual purposes.* We planned an evening to do it. We played some music on the rooftop, invited a few people over (Jaya's friends), and lit up the whole place to create the right environment. When I say we, I mean mostly Jaya did it, I did whatever little I was told to.

After I gulped down the pill, I sat next to the speakers gazing up at the sky. Till there was no one — just me, and the never-ending vastness of space. It terrified me and soothed me, all at once. *What if the sky were to fall down and envelop me in its darkness, till I was a part of it? — nothing and everything, at the same time.*

Far away, I could hear people dancing and laughing. I felt the reverberations of the music on the concrete. *If the sky were to come down on me now, crush my lungs, extinguish all this emptiness, and fill it with whatever the cosmos is made up of, I would gladly accept it.*

Every day passed in haze. Jaya chimed about her kid cousin who was coming to visit them in the city. People in the office talked about the shows they had watched at home or what they had done with their partners. My father talked about how he was nearing death. The only interesting thing that happened were the snippets of conversations I heard on the local train. If only rarely, and briefly. Then one day, it really happened. My father passed away.

We went to burn his body in the late hours of dusk. As I watched him go up in flames, it occurred to me that I was still alone — as my father had stated; and a certain sense of loneliness pervaded me, one that hadn't been there before. Like I mentioned earlier, I didn't mind being alone.

Later, the lawyer told me he had left everything to his second wife — except for a box of my belongings. They were mainly old books and trophies. I was surprised that that he had even kept them all these years. I didn't bother perusing the box and pushed it under my bed. That night I dreamt that I was back on the overcrowded platform, still trying to stop my father, but before I could scream for him, he turned around and looked at me. A moment passed between us. No words were exchanged. Then he just turned away and walked off. Just like that. Jaya had a full eight-hour sleep that night.

Jaya was, however, panicking about what she would gift her cousin. Both she and her boyfriend did not seem to gauge the kid's age or the appropriate toy for him. That day I was sitting by the balcony wondering what it would be like to casually jump off when she interrupted me to ask me silly questions about what to gift. After much deliberation, (mainly on her side, to herself,) I offered her the box of my childhood belongings — just to shut her up.

Though initially sceptical, she (and I) was surprised to see the mint condition things were in. As she went through the toys, I looked at the books. I could categorise these books according to the phases I went through in my life. Mystery novels to books of poetry, western philosophy, and leftist political novels. I wondered if the person who read these books was the same person standing here. *Probably not.*

That's when I saw it. Hard bound in leather, with the words inscribed on it in gold. 'Irzaya.' Sudden flashes of images went through my head. My mother's fingers in my hair, a makeshift tent we had camped out of on the roof when I was six, her growing thinner and frailer, slowly disappearing before my eyes into the summer sun. Before I knew it, gone.

I quickly felt something rise up my stomach to my throat. I was going to hurl. I excused myself and went to the washroom. There on the bathroom mirror I saw that my entire face was flushed. I was surprised to see hot tears streaming down my cheeks. Still nauseated I looked down into the sink, focused on a single spot with all my might.

Jaya, in the meanwhile, had found what she was looking for and screamed for me in her shrill voice. I kept trying to wipe the tears, but they kept coming. I wanted to lay on the floor and weep. I didn't know what had happened — suddenly, the whole world had shifted from beneath my feet just for a second and put itself back to the way it was. But that one second was enough.

Everything had shifted.

Jaya called again and I ignored her. She eventually found me on the bathroom floor weeping into the white tiles. She got so worried that she called her boyfriend over, or maybe he was already there camping in her room. He carried me to my room like a baby while she watched over and tucked me into my bed. I was still crying. She hushed and petted me. They took the box out and shut the lights on their way. Jaya could be really understanding about these things, I really was lucky to have her.

That night I dreamt of someone who looked like my mother. She was holding me in her arms. I was an infant in the dream. I looked down beneath me and there was just darkness down there, endless darkness, the kind where stars were born out of and faded into; and I knew at once. When I looked into her eyes, I asked her if it would be scary down there and she said no, *it would be like falling asleep.*

10

Surrounded Assurance

by Jigyasa Tandon

(TW: Sexual abuse)

Dear Parineeta,

Being an elder sister, I am writing this letter to you since you are moving to a new city. I hope it helps you and that you gain insight and inspiration from it.

I had recently changed cities for work, touring the country 360 degrees. With a perspective of judging people from their clothing to actions, I guess I retained that aspect in common with my surrounding, but other parameters greatly differed for me! The tune they fixed their steps to and the steps they followed were completely different. And, in a diverse country, heterogeneity carries loopholes and so does adult freedom. But, people with two eyes, two ears, one nose, and one mouth make a holism everywhere; perpetually acting a similar way, even with the distinction of culture and methods.

Anyway, the inspired youth across the world actively look for assets of negativity to pull themselves into pop culture; thus, arrogance, drugs, cigarettes, alcohol, and rebellious behaviour are common. Maybe it's a modern movement to define freedom to people. I was no different, but a part of the league. Job, career, education, the standard of living, communication — all mattered, but being rebellious was my own mark of honour!

Now, I stood in a city where I was miles away from my personal instructors of societal defiance; independent and free to explore the possibilities; to know the world better. So, every day after work, I used to hit a cafe or a bar and made notes to be a part of the city. There were trance moments for me. While the quietness of a cafe gave chills running through spines, the high rush of the bar gave peace. And in between, through GPS directions, life happened.

This was exactly the way I came across friends, and my college friend's mate. Having familiarity and cultural resemblance, we had hit it up together, quite quickly. From common plans to chilling, it was all turning into a routine. And in this race to make the unknown city dance to my tune, I skipped the beat of wild animal actions.

Since, as a country, we are losing jungles and greens, the animals are making comfortable homes within us. And for us to be a part of upright social modernity, we do away from that sight believing that climate activism will make things right. Facts and believed facts need a check.

I was then invited to a house party and asked to stay back. Because that is abiding by the rules of the 'All Young Social Rebellion Movement.' But there's a catch to it, are we choosing humans or hooligans to be part of the movement? Because that, I guess, was the night of battles, putting out, and rage in the open.

While some were busy numbing their cognitions, some were in a state of a standstill, and some being highly functioning — there was a wolf who rested his eyes upon me. While people started leaving, his night started to grow stronger. Finding the appropriate time, the full moon, his time for attack seemed perfect.

The next thing that happened was a morning with a naked, bruised, painted red with cig marks and added colours of tied hands. The tears seemed to have dried up. Episode ended.

Having a stretched day of creativity in mental health, I found myself, numbed with a robotic body working for her passion. The evening seemed to be thick, possessing a change of dynamics. I churned it to make it fluid. With an irritating feeling and long face, I went to a cafe to attend an open mic. I even registered to speak a poem aloud.

The next 3 hours were the longest and the most difficult hours for me; numb, lost self-esteem, head lowered with shame, words forming poems relating the pain, and of course, a constant urge to smoke.

Continued mind chatter had put out of focus a man who'd been trying to initiate a conversation with me to know whether everything was okay. His chance to perform came and that was when I took notice of him. He had familiarity. But his presence had elegance and serenity, too. I was so scared that I couldn't lay my eyes on him.

The program came to an end. The smoke deal had to burst out. But, hey, the familiar guy was here; he was around. *Should I ask him to join in? Um…*

'Hey, Delhi guy, you smoke? Wanna join me?'

'Yes,' he answered. A small conversation happened, one of getting to know the formal backgrounds. In between, there were snippet slidings of who we were, apart from that professional identity. I think it was deliberate intention? What do you think? On finishing our smoke and biting into extra time, we departed for the evening.

I spent that whole night on the terrace crying for me, for God to come, show his presence and end the trail of my deceptive relationships. Relationships with sexual harassment and questioning morality.

In my heart, I had his image; it made a continued appearance. I denied acceptance. It felt all wrong, every sign and sense of it. The ideals and media terms were occurring parallelly to confirm and validate it.

The next day was professionally important. I had my chance to make the first impression, to spill my skills out to my guides. I was focused on preparing for it. At around 2, he messaged:

Wanna catch up where we left yesterday? I felt intrigued by your knowledge and a lot of discussions are waiting to happen...

Not having saved his number yet jumbled, I answered:

Yeah, okay, meet you at 5.

The training session ended at 6:45 pm. I checked my phone — there were only 2 missed calls. I called back in a hurry to confirm if everything was okay.

He smiled and answered, 'I'm waiting.' I felt relieved.

That day, I reached the place at 7:45 pm. (He stood there with a hand extended to propose. Oh, sorry.) He stood there greeting me, and had looked forward to having conversation and tea, waiting since 4:30 pm.

It was that 'moment' which made me realise that he was the god in disguise, and his presence in my life was all the difference I had prayed to be assured of.

That was my encounter with a stranger, which is turning out to mean life to me now.

But then, it was only a realisation that went rippling through my heart, and butterflies in the stomach. It was yet to be communicated — and that needed time. My body still was afresh with the retirement from the violent depression. And this man who may appear like God had to be tested for sound and action.

The evening began as a general discussion, with waves of smoke and a breeze of tea; some topics of interest came up, but what held us through was a dream of Freud.

In the following weeks, exchange of words started with worldly materials, of opportunities, of talent. While I realised his power to spell hope to people struggling, he felt my bold oration to motivate people to achieve their goals upright. We had few moments of conflict too on the road, but I won't lie, I love them. Yes, people find it weird, but for me, it's a powerful and liberating thing. To express and let express; and in the pond, fish for a conclusion.

This was now a routine. Slowly, the strong-headedness was being replaced with light talks, and there was a little stupidity, and childish dreams of finding ways to pop in — to draw each other closer. Now the belief was affirmative, that he was being the being I wanted in life; a realisation that happened between the random road-trips to watch the sunrise, roadside eateries, his college's coffee shop, and other things.

The constant non-crashing idea of respect, identity, and choice was maintained, somehow, rather unspoken it was. This was quite safe and pacifying. In part, it was all brewing in friendship, to know each other, better than jumping into a relationship or pouncing upon for bitten grave seemed well. This could be really a deciding factor for continuing the friendship or starting the new chapter.

A few months later, while we were on his bike on the way to my office, which was seemingly a differed place from normal offices. He asked me, 'Lolita, I see you making your contribution, to create a difference in society — which excites me, because you don't make special efforts. You do things your way. But the very nature of your work makes you feel proud every day that you did something differently. And now, I want the same for my life, too

— and to close the difference between us, each day. What do you think of that addition to your life?'

The chapter began with a live-in in the city of known unknowns, having every possibility of inviting judgment. But their houses were run by people like us, so they ended up being the judgemental advisors to relationships. Telling us about the ups and downs, and how the girl needs to build a little home.

With this, challenges became social security; and mental awareness of needs and choices were a helpful reminder to sustain the relationship, and housing in the hearts forward.

Today, we live in different cities and it's four years to our relationship. Stability and surety hold us together. With the pressure building-up on my approaching the age of wedlock, the age-difference between us is a new topic for discussion.

But, since he's the stranger that drives my story of love, I am still waiting for him to start the car and define the next destination.

Keep this in mind, hardly older people tell us of stories like these happening around. But the possibilities never die. I am there, for your stories. Take care.

Regards,

Lolita

11

Rose Coloured Glasses

by Sindhuja Sarasram

I've been catfished.

I've been catfished and I think I led myself right into the trap. That's the thought I sat with, for about a minute, trying to make sense of everything. Before I flipped the bird, threw back the seat, and stormed off.

I am so angry I could cry. My nostrils flare, but good thing about the face mask is this screen hiding my emotions. I keep walking, as I've been, from when I walked out of the restaurant. *Fucking tears.* I blink back and check my phone to find directions to Saket station. It's hard to focus. I bang right between the shoulders of a couple walking in the opposite direction. 'Bro, watch where you're going!'

'Sorry. Sorry.' I apologize, turning my face away. *Men don't cry.* I don't want to be judged, not today. But I'm not crying; not about excitedly dropping off Freddy and Ziggy over at my careless brother's place; or about having spent half of my last pay check on the new casual jacket I'm wearing. But I am – over the mental energy and emotions spent through the course of 6 long months that were building up to this day. This moment. One of anticipation, and as apparent now — one of betrayal. Over the person who is not who I thought they were.

A brittle laugh escapes me. To think that I was the one who initiated conversation.

***

It all started on social media during the complete National lockdown. Everyone and their woke parents had become content creators and influencers. When not overworked to my bones, I spent my lonesome nights scrolling through Instagram. Not that I had complaints about work — I loved my job, and it was a huge distraction from my personal life, or the lack of one.

My friend Meena often kept sharing deep messages through relatable quotes from this one account that went by: its.Rosey.AF

In my recently single state, I craved for some looking. One night, I tapped on the profile. It had a pouty selfie with wildly curly shoulder-length hair shadowing half the features, while the other part of the face was covered with a big, pink, heart-shaped lens.

The description read:

Ros A Ferreira

Artist

Thanks for asking about my day! How's yours?

A li'l bit better with my clouds, unicorn, and glittery poop. I hope?

Holy... There were about 7000 followers to this account. The grid was full of quotes in various experimental fonts, with a dominantly pink-coloured cloud background. The witty username and the bio pulled me in. And I came across a story.

This stranger was seated on the couch between the two others fighting over a TV remote. With arms shrugging, they gestured at the camera. There was a poll:

Haalp! I need to settle the dispute between these two women before they kill me in my sleep. The office or F.R.I.E.N.D.S?

I went ahead and wrote: Neither. Both shows like to stereotype anything that's not White, American or Straight!

The response was immediate: Damn straight! (Pun intended) Sigh, my flatmates!

Me: Haha! I'm glad I'm not living with them...

Ros: Way to rub it in!

Me: Just curious, do you really like pink so much?

Ros: Aha, now see who's stereotyping...! And who says it's pink?

Me: Touché! Wait, Ah, so... it's the colour 'Rose' then?

Ros: Now you get it!

Me: So, you are admitting that all that toxic positivity you're posting only passes through your rose-coloured filter? I'd felt smart sending that.

Ros: Go through my posts and share even one thing that feels toxic back to me. Go on...

Seriously? I thought before scanning the posts. I scrolled down, one after the other, and they all went like:

It's okay to not be okay

It's okay to cry sometimes

All vibes are welcome here

And I gave up. Swallowing my pride, I messaged after giving it some thought over the next afternoon: I'm sorry. I think I really hate that colour, so I didn't actually see the words for what they mean. Really, I am sorry.

Apology accepted. And you're not the first person to mansplain me this, but you're the first one to apologize.

I cringed at my own words from before.

Really? I'm surprised you don't block accounts who troll you.

It was embarrassing, how I was now one of *them*.

Well, now I got you to see the truth, didn't I?

And that Saturday night in July, our conversation stretched out until daylight. We discussed about everything including our favourite TV shows, characters, where we saw ourselves at the end of the pandemic, our past relationships, what kept us awake at night, and what made us happy.

I think this conversation has made my day! my phone pinged. Like I needed the notification tone, when all the while, my phone had been glued to my hand, the chat screen glowing on my face in the dark. I eagerly anticipated the next text, emoji, or GIF. I felt a connection like none other before; and I had been caught hook, line and sinker. Because, what followed the conversation was me cyber-stalking every profile this person ever had through all social-media platforms — which wasn't a lot. There was just a twitter account that pretty much mirrored the Instagram posts.

There were a lot of illustrated posters which were, of course, reflective of Ros's work as a graphic designer in an uptown studio in Colaba, Mumbai — knowledge I'd become privy to, during the night. Among all the fluffy pink clouds, there were some profile pictures — few and far between; with dogs, in artsy lighting, in paint — the hair always taking centre-stage, and the face mostly hidden. Back then, I think the mystery was overly appealing to me. Also, I could care less about people's looks; what their hearts were made of, that's what mattered to me.

Scrolling through, I accidentally pressed *like*. On the first post on the account, from about a year before. *MotherF.* Now Ros would surely know that I was stalking. But then I thought, *so what if it's seen that way? I am interested, aren't I*? So, I then proceeded to comment on it: OMG, yes. I totally get it!

Over the next few days, our conversations helped me through my demanding work hours. I thought I finally had met someone who understood me and whom I could vent to, without a filter. It was just a friendship, but I had a feeling that the need for more was mutual.

Some nights were casual questions like: Maggie with ketchup or without?

The reply would be instant: Does it matter? If each of us prefers it differently?

Me: Right answer!

Ros: Wait, was that a trick question? HA. Haha ha. I've got one for you...

Waiting with bated breath!

Ros: Who would you rather? Your boss or your brother's girlfriend?

Me: No. NOOOOOO! I told you I hate both of them! And you ask this knowing me?!

A GIF of a little girl's evil laugh came as a reply.

Me: That's cute. Looks like you. Really, being the same height n all...

Ros: That was a cheap shot, Ronak. Thought you to be so intelligent and shit. All that Viper and Mamba you keep talking about, with that nerdy brain of yours.

Me: It's PYTHON!

Ros: Okay, well. Python — your tiny IQ just got swallowed by one.

After a minute, another text followed: BOOM! Roasted.

I was comfortable with the texting. Hell, I loved texting. As I always hadn't an easy way with speaking, I preferred writing over calls; because they allowed me time to compose my thoughts well. And with Ros, it was so very easy that I didn't even have to think so much.

There was a story with a picture of Ros's silhouette against the evening sky. There was nothing seductive about it except the hungry look in the eyes. The caption read 'Thinking of you…'

Me: Thinking of all your 10k fanboys?

Ros: Aww, you're cute. And who says there are just boys...?

As I flipped my calendar from August to September, casual talk turned into real flirtation, and our conversations moved from Instagram to WhatsApp.

One of the lonelier nights, I wrote: Would you date me?

With immediate regret, I deleted it. But I got a reply: In a heartbeat! Would you, though?

Me: Why do I have to date somebody like myself when I already have me?

I wrote again, Kidding

And another: Would you go on a real date with me before the new year?

I saw the minute long three dots and the silence before the reply popped: *Yes!*

We, finally, officially, were dating long-distance in October. Phone-calls were still not a thing, but we had made plans to meet, in the flesh, on New Year's Eve. I chose that occasion because I wanted to show how important it was for me. So, we finally decided that Ros would fly out to meet me in Delhi and I'd take care of the itinerary for the whole weekend.

On my birthday in November, I received a pink t-shirt with a tacky, printed quote that had me laughing every time I looked at it.

***

Back in the metro concourse as I wait impatiently for my train, I see him again. Dragging his trolley bag through the slippery granite flooring of the platform opposite me, at the pace of guilt, face downcast.

One night before the false relationship even began, heavily triggered by my ex's lovey-dovey photos I had drunk-dialled Ros several times to not have them answered. I had even sent a cringey, needy text.

I need you, please!

My calls were returned much later. And receiving it, I vomited everything that weighed on my chest. At dawn, exhausted and empty, but also feeling lighter, I sleep to the rhythmic sound of Ros breathing on the other end. It truly felt like Ros had been holding my hand through it all. *It was all a lie.*

I watch him sit down, only to get up again and move farther along, having seen me. *Good.* I look down at my phone to go through that wretched Instagram profile to figure it out. One last time, before I block him. *How did I miss the signs?* There were all the photos and videos we exchanged. Correction, photos we both shared; videos that only I shared. *Huh.*

I scroll through to that first comment I had posted. It was under this image of Ros holding a poster that read:

'There is only one way to look at things until someone shows us how to look at them with different eyes.' – Pablo Picasso

I pull down and read the caption under the picture and the blood drains from my face. What I believed he hid from me, was plainly stated there. Reading those words again, I have an epiphany.

And I realise the irony of the quoted words, and my current predicament; *I* was not catfished, I was just somebody who made gross assumptions.

Everything looks fuzzy. Licking my dry lips, I stare at that comment I'm made under that text, over 10 months ago:

OMG, yes. I totally get it! More power to you!

I now know that I'd not understood what I was acknowledging when I stated that I related to him; I hadn't, really.

And I think back to all our interactions. *Ros not picking my calls on that drunken night... his silence as I poured my heart out... when he hesitatingly texted if I'd date somebody like him...* All that time. He must have thought that I was a person who looked at him just the same — as a normal nice man, into other men, like I am.

But he is nice, and I am not. Rather, I am a biased guy that flaked on their date, after realising that they were speech impaired. I sink my elbows into my knees and pull at my hair. *What am I?*

Startling my co-travellers waiting on the bench, I jump from my seat and look across the tracks. But the halting train on the other side blocks my view of where Ros was seated. I know I have to be quick— he'll surely leave on that train.

I do a quick google search and look up to see the train come to a halt. The doors open, and there's a flow of people in and out. In their midst, I spot his pink sweater, luckily. I will him to look up, and he does, answering my prayers.

I quickly make a gesture with my right fist making a circle against my chest, meaning sorry, according to somebody on YouTube. I hope they are right. Ros gives me a slight nod. And the train starts. *Shit.*

Running along the length of the platform to keep up with the train, I unzip and shrug off my jacket and strip down to my t-shirt. Understanding dawns on Ros's face and I discern the twinkle in his eyes, and he starts to shake with laughter. But I don't miss the sadness behind them. That look makes me feel worser than I did an hour ago when I thought I'd been used.

And that's all I see before the security drags me away from the platform edge, 'Sir, what are you doing?! Step back, the train is approaching.'

The front of the pink T-shirt I'm wearing reads:

Code me like I'm one of your French girls.

The back, with pride colours, reads: Love, Rosey.

'Yes, yes. Okay.'

And I know right there that I'm not worthy of that love. And that I'm not ready for it, having several things to figure out, starting with my own prejudices. *Thank you for the lesson. I hope you find somebody worth your time.*

12

Known Stranger

by Kongkona Baishya

It took her a while to reach the address following Google Maps. The tiny pointers and the directions on the phone display really stressed her eyes out; the scorching October sun made it a bit exhausting for her as it glared on her screen. She took the lift, combed through the corridors, and finally found her destination. Korobi was feeling excited and nervous at the same time.

There was a light buzz inside the hall; chairs were arranged in perfect alignment facing a solid mosaic-tiled stage. Korobi took a seat, relaxed her muscles, and threw a glance at her surroundings. Everyone inside the room was an aspiring actor and so was Korobi. She'd found out about the Acting Workshop and decided to give it a shot. Well, the decision was not that easy, especially for a woman of 33. *But, better late than never.*

There was still half an hour to go and Korobi just hated the waiting. She was all by herself, so she decided to venture outside. She stepped out to admire the neatly pruned garden and the cold breeze. There was a coffee station inside the campus, and she bought herself a cup. The first warm sip was enough to stimulate her nerves. She was enjoying this novel approach to life she determined for herself. A bad breakup, a mundane life routine, and societal expectations had drained the last ounce of her mental peace. So, she resolved to take matters into her own hands; she dug up her buried dream — the one she had in her teens that later died at the hands of familial responsibilities.

A loud honk broke her string of thoughts. A white colour SUV drove by, as if it hardly cared about the rules of the road. Korobi hated such jerks who thought they owned the road. A young man hopped off; all clad in black. She peeked a glance at his chauvinist, superior conviction; she despised such looks.

Korobi left the spot and went inside the hall. The seats were almost full. The lighting arrangements added a different feel to the place. The workshop began. She took a deep sigh, all set to delve deep into this world of art and acting. However, a small part of her brain seemed to be obsessed with that black-clad guy.

First, it was the welcome speech by the organisers, later followed by introductions from all the participants — then they were divided into many groups, each assigned with preparing a piece from popular novels, from short stories, or from any of the epics. All the members of Korobi's group were younger than her, and perhaps, that made the equation a bit odd. Korobi picked a character with few dialogues since her venture into this world was very fresh.

Korobi managed to look unperturbed through her group's reading and watched the others — some of them were spectacular. She realised that was only a warm-up. A few more group exercises later, suddenly, that man from earlier walked onto the stage. Korobi felt a bit inquisitive. Three participants were called each time; they were given a situation without any dialogues and were asked to improvise until they emoted the required emotion and justified the plot.

After each piece, he breezily pointed out the flaws and areas for improvement to each team. Korobi waited for her turn; Because everybody else seemed to have already formed groups of three, except her, she remained by herself at the end. And so, Korobi was called up alone. Her heart thumped, and she became conscious as she walked onto the stage, with innumerable eyes resting on her. She held her fear within, trying very hard not to appear so obvious.

'Korobi Choudhury, right?' spoke that intense voice.

'Yes,' Korobi was cautious not to sound too strung up.

'Looks like you have to do your piece with me. Are you ready?'

She tried processing what he said and the more she tried, she could feel her ears getting warm. She wasn't ready for this interaction yet, definitely not on her first day at the workshop. Korobi side-eyed the audience staring at her. She could feel a nervous ball rolling inside her stomach and tried hard to remain composed.

'Yeah,' replied Korobi calmly.

'Fine...so let's assume you're madly in love with me.'

'Pardon?' Korobi blurted and the very next moment, she felt extremely embarrassed.

Abhimanyu smiled.

'ASSUME,' he stretched the word and continued, 'and you finally decide to say it… but also, you're an introvert. Now, convey your feelings to the love of your life in an *explicit* way. I am Abhimanyu, Abhimanyu Sarma, in case you didn't hear me earlier — address me by the name. Alright?"

Korobi nodded her head and took a deep breath.

The microphone made a noise as it was being adjusted.

Korobi started.

'Abhi… Abhimanyu, I need to tell you something before I leave.'

'Leave? Where to…?'

'For Delhi... for my internship. But there is something I must tell you... Now, right now — before I lose my mind.'

'Yes...,' Abhimanyu seemed to enjoy the way the act was progressing. His composed facade messed up with her head. For a moment she felt she would blow it, but she kept her focus.

Korobi let her heart speak. She channelled the weight of the past and brought it to the surface.

'It hurts me when I see these pretty girls hitting on you... and you just give them more reasons to do so.'

'More reasons?'

'Yes... your smile — that one smile,' Korobi looked straight into Abhimanyu's eyes, this time as if trying to read it.

'My smile?'

'Yes... the one thing I fall for, every time I see... your soulful smile.'

'But... Since when do you have feelings for me?' Abhimanyu took a step towards her as he shifted the tone of his voice to a deeper one. Korobi felt like she was struggling in a vast ocean of thoughts, trying to find the right thing to say.

'I don't know — feels like from eternity... it's so deep that I can see past the pain your smile holds.'

'Korobi... I don't see you as a woman... you're still that two-pony-tailed, obedient, and polite girl to me...'

'I know... I know the way I am... and I know the way you are. But I must confess it before I leave... Maybe, this will be our last conversation.' She paused, 'Life may flow in a different direction, but I will remember this moment, even if it's the last... I love you — always have, from the time I have come to know you.'

Korobi thought he would end the scene there, but Abhimanyu continued.

'And, what if I hurt you today?'

She tried to give the best reply. 'You can't... because I won't give you that power. All I know that I love you and no one can love you the way I do.'

'What if I can't love you back?'

'It's alright; like I said, you can't hurt me. Someday, I might get over you — however long that takes… I hope my love for me will be enough.' she paused, 'Goodbye.'

There was a pin drop silence and Abhimanyu seemed caught up.

'The act is over,' Korobi questioned, 'Right?'

'Oh, yes… Wow,' Abhimanyu clapped. The hall thudded with claps. Korobi breathed with relief; she was happy, her spirit elevated.

Outside the hall, the other participants congratulated her. Korobi thanked everyone, with genuine warmth. She adjusted her tote bag and walked out. A blaring honk from behind startled her. She moved aside to make way for the car to pass by, but it halted beside her. Abhimanyu rolled down the window and looked at Korobi.

'Korobi, hi… let me give you a lift,' offered Abhimanyu. Korobi hesitated.

'It's okay… Come on.'

Accepting the offer, Korobi climbed in and gave a polite smile.

'So, Korobi... have you tried auditioning?'

'No…' replied Korobi faintly.

'Oh…you should!'

'Actually, this is my first time — on any stage.'

'Really?! It was very good.' He looked amazed. Korobi smiled.

And that's how everything started.

Korobi would look forward to each day of the workshop, full of anticipation. She felt as if she was opening up to a whole new world, exploring possibilities out there. She found her true guide in him. Abhimanyu was a saviour and a charmer who could literally make everything comfortable for her. Korobi often thought about how she despised him the first time she laid eyes on him. She judged the book by its cover, and she was wrong.

Korobi enjoyed his company. Small conversation soon led to bigger ones: soulful, honest, and often, a blend of wit and humour. Abhimanyu would often share script-writing sessions with her virtually and it would continue late into the night. They soon started meeting outside the workshop: in his office or her house.

One evening, as they were deeply engrossed in their writing, there was a power outage due to stormy weather; Korobi lit the candles she stocked for emergency. She let the cold breeze swipe in through a half-open windowpane. As she was adjusting the candle stand, she saw Abhimanyu looking at her, smitten. Her heart fluttered a little.

'Sorry, the back-up is out as well… Do you want some tea?' Korobi tried to fill up the silence.

'Yeah, tea… Sure,' Abhimanyu was caught off-guard.

Korobi made her special ginger-tea — hot and aromatic.

'So, what are you? A tea girl?' Abhimanyu teased her, as he took the first sip.

'Hmm, I don't know… you can't actually take the tea out of an Assamese, you see — it runs in our veins,' Korobi laughed as she finished.

'That's funny… you're funny, but I find you cute… with all your reasoning and — I don't know, your particular reactions to particular situations. I just find everything cute,' Abhimanyu delicately touched a strand of her hair with his long fingers and kept it hooked on her right ear. Korobi shivered a little. He approached her for a kiss, and before she realised, she was in his arms.

They ended up sharing everything: body, mind, fears, dreams, and doubts. Life was finally turning out to be full of passion, and Abhimanyu only added more meaning to it. Whenever she came to think of a reason, she found two: her love for her newly found talent and her love for him. She was loving it all — even his intimidation.

Abhimanyu had marked himself in her life plan: present, future, and ever after. She was all drenched in the rain of love until one day he broke that illusion of hers. It was in the urge of a moment, that Korobi asked him where he saw her in his future. She was positive and excited to hear his answer, but he went numb; it took him a few minutes to find an answer.

'I… it's just — I haven't thought about us in that way, Korobi. I mean, time changes, so do people. And what if I change…?' he was brutally honest, 'I don't want to hurt you.'

Korobi could feel her heart pounding, and her eyes stung. Her world had capsized, and the pain was excruciating. She grabbed her bag and sprinted out of his office as fast as she could. But with her vision blurred by tears, she couldn't even find her way out.

They didn't talk for months. Every now and then she tried outlets to channelize her pain. Korobi went to a bunch of auditions, applied for internships in creative writing; and when she got selected for one, she knew she had to take it. She knew escaping wasn't good enough, so she vowed to give herself a chance: a chance at healing and accepting the pain, no matter how deep it was.

As Korobi waited for her flight, she reflected over many things. She felt the vibration in her bag and took out the phone.

It was Abhimanyu, and she wasn't ready for the conversation. She reluctantly received the call.

'Where are you...?' Abhimanyu sounded curious.

'Leaving...'

'Leaving? Where?'

There was a prolonged silence at both the ends.

'Don't bother yourself with that,' she said in a measured tone.

'Hey, Korobi. Listen to me, you don't have to do this, for me... Look, I'm extremely sorry...'

'S... Sorry? Sorry for what?' she stammered. A storm was raging inside her.

'Sorry for letting you believe that I had feelings for you.' It felt like Abhimanyu was ready with the response. All he wanted was to unburden his sense of guilt. The storm broke out; Korobi couldn't hold it in any longer.

'Then what was it?' she demanded to know.

'It's so hard to explain... maybe it was just a moment of emotional weakness,' blurted Abhimanyu.

Korobi felt a pang inside her. 'Why ME? I was just happy in my space... never asked you for anything... Then, why me?'

'I never thought things will turn out this way — that you will end up falling in love.' said Abhimanyu.

Korobi laughed, 'Isn't that ironic... You were the first to approach me, you were the first to exhibit all the signs, and to ask what I felt for you — and I showed you! But you never felt the same, everything was so easy for you...' She was not sure if any of it made sense to him; everything she was afraid of expressing rushed out of her; her voice broke at the end. 'Do you have any idea how much it hurts? How humiliating it is?'

'I'm sorry... you know, the way I am...'

'Yes... and I know the way I am... and even if it's the last thing I want to say,' Thinking of the familiarity of the moment, and words spoken, in a different place, at a different time — to the same recipient, Korobi smiled to herself ruefully. She could feel each and every word she said, 'I do love you and no one can love you the way I do.'

'Korobi, please, don't leave. I am ready to take responsibility...'

This was the last of the humiliation she could take. 'Mr. Abhimanyu Sarma, I'm not a mistake that you will take responsibility for. Goodbye.'

Korobi disconnected the call. She breathed out the pain whooshing out of her chest and lump in her throat. She started walking towards the departure gates.

On the plane, Korobi took a deep sigh, letting her guard down as she leaned back on her seat. A hot trail of water burned her cheek. She kept ruminating her first meeting with Abhimanyu.

Sometimes it might seem difficult to let go of someone you love so deeply, but you know you must — because it would be wrong to give someone that power to control your emotions, your mind, and your heart. Her own written words came back to strengthen her resolve. *In fact, it would be better to be a known stranger.*

The final announcement was done, and the flight took off. Korobi closed her eyes, only to open and witness a new beginning.

PART 4

// WHAT IF GOD WAS ONE OF US //

Touchstones of the ages

13

The Mayor of Bandra

by Prerna Singh

In the June of 2012, while it was summer in most parts of the country, it was Leela's first rendezvous with the Bombay monsoons. Yes, she still prefers to call it 'Bombay.'

Leela had finally moved to the city she always hoped to work in as a corporate lawyer. She was all of 24, bright, ambitious and quite independent for her age, when she switched cities. While she had the experience of living on her own in Bangalore and Delhi, moving to the Maximum City can nevertheless be overwhelming for anyone. And so was it for her. Thankfully, the organisation she worked for, and her colleagues extended all kinds of support to her when she arrived in Bombay — arranging her airport pick-up, setting- up her workstation, ordering for a great welcome lunch, and even making arrangements to accommodate her bags in office till she found a place of her own.

Leela had planned to stay at her friend's place for the first two weeks upon her arrival to the city, factoring in the time that she would require to freeze upon an apartment for herself. However, her first two days of crazy commute to office in the said monsoons prompted her to expedite the apartment search. One must experience the monsoons in Bombay to know how generous the Rain Gods could be.

Leela was always certain she wanted to stay close to her workplace but after getting soaked for two consecutive days, she revised her accommodation search parameter to: 'in the same area as the office.' There were many such revisions vis-à-vis her expectations and what Bombay had to offer instead. For instance, within two days of scouting, 'apartment' search became 'room' search, courtesy- Bombay rentals.

On her third day at work, a partially sunny one, she proactively decided to use her lunch time to explore the accommodations available in the vicinity through a broker. She searched online for contacts of some local brokers in Khar and made her first call to a broker named Olvin Fobler.

'Hi. My name is Leela. Am I speaking to Mr. Olvin Fobler?'

'Hello. *Hello*. Yes, this is Olvin. Please tell me.'

The man had a warm, husky voice with a sophisticated diction unique only to him. When Leela made that call, she was not prepared to hear such a refined man for a broker.

'...Yes, Mr Fobler, that's right. I want an independent place — and not on sharing basis.'

'Alright. Let me get back to you in a couple of hours.'

'Thank you, Mr. Fobler. I would like to move in as soon as possible... So, it'll be great if you could show me some options by today — I'll wait for your call.'

She discussed her budget and requirements with him at length and was hoping to hear back from him by noon. He called her back an hour or so later.

'Hello. Hello, Olvin here.' *He would always say hello twice. That was archetypal Olvin Fobler for you.*

'I can show you two places this afternoon. I have one more place on my mind that may suit you — but I am not sure if the owner will be available to show it today. Uh... Anyway, we can see that some other day, maybe. If you wish to see the other two places today, I could meet you around 1 p.m. at your office... Please, let me know if that's convenient for you.'

They agreed to meet up at the time proposed by Olvin Fobler. Leela was intrepid enough a woman, however given her conditioning, hearsay experiences from friends and acquaintances in other cities, and also the fact that she had moved from Delhi (a city infamous for incidents, particularly with women) she was slightly apprehensive about being picked up by a stranger.

At the same time, she was too new to the organisation to ask anyone to accompany her in accommodation search as that felt like a personal favour. So, while a tad hesitant, she followed her instinct and stepped down to meet Mr. Fobler at 1 p.m. outside her office. He was there before time, patiently waiting for the clock to tick 1 and just as she was coming out of the elevator, her phone started to ring. Within seconds, both of them realised they were facing each other.

'Hi. Hi. You must be Leela.' He greeted, while they shook hands.

Leela had imagined him to be a middle-aged fellow but there he was, standing firm, 6-feet and 4-inches tall with a broad build — a bald-headed man, clad in a striped polo shirt, beige pleated trousers, and Nike shoes. At 74, he adorned the best of smiles. In many ways, he defined the spirit of Bombay for Leela. Like the city, he was a fine blend of the old-world charm and the contemporary realm.

'Shall we?' Fobler asked Leela as he waited for her to step inside the auto-rikshaw he had hired for them.

'Sure.'

'Please, please.' He gave her way and requested her to step in before him.

A thorough gentleman, he was suave, charming, eloquent, and exceptionally courteous. Leela was instantly at ease in his company and in fact, started to revel in it within minutes of meeting him.

There are some extraordinary moments in life when you feel strongly connected to the person you have hardly spent any time with, unless of course you are completely shut to the ways of the universe; this was one such exceptional moment for Leela.

Incidentally, it was during the same rikshaw ride with Mr. Fobler that Leela caught the first glimpse of the Arabian Sea on Carter Road — her first since she had landed in Bombay.

'Wow! Was I this close to the sea!?' exclaimed Leela.

'Oh yes, my friend. This is the Carter Road promenade.'

'What a spectacular view! I'd love to jog here.'

'You jog! That's good. Would you like to stop, and see?'

Leela was itching to say a yes with double 'S's but was hesitant considering that Mr. Fobler would have lost out on his time if they stopped by, so she didn't say anything. By then, Mr. Fobler on his own accord said, 'Let's stop and show you around,' and asked the rikshaw driver to halt.

In those two hours that she was with Mr. Fobler, he showed her the best of his world, the best of Bombay he knew — the best of Bandra, Khar.

'Since you like to jog, you cannot *not* see the Jogger's Park. I have been walking there for years now.'

'That sounds great, Mr. Fobler.' And just like that, he ended up showing her the best of cafes, pubs, and gymkhanas of Bandra and Khar, or at least the ones that he thought were worthy enough.

'You should have cupcakes from here sometime,' Fobler told Leela as they passed by *Candies*, which in later months happened to be frequented by Leela.

While he showed some of these places to her when they were on route to see one of the accommodations, he also went out of his way to show her the other locales such as the Pali Hill, Linking Road, and so on. This kind gesture was without even knowing if Leela would like any of the accommodations he was showing her in the capacity of a broker. He was himself, right from the time they met, and his zeal for life was not only apparent but also contagious.

By now, Leela had begun to fall for the city; she couldn't wait to start her life here. To Mr. Fobler's disbelief, Leela decided to stay in the accommodation that he least expected her to like. So much so, that he was not even willing to show it to her.

'It's not up to your standards, my friend.'

'Please Mr. Fobler, I would still like to see it. Just in case I happen to like it — I'll be at a walking distance from my workplace.'

'Alright, let me arrange for the keys — if you insist. I see that you are keen on making me burn extra calories today.'

'Oh, no. Absolutely not. I'll quickly climb and have a look at it myself. Don't worry! Please don't take the trouble of climbing so many floors just to show me the room.'

But Fobler being Fobler, of course, accompanied Leela in the herculean task of climbing that inconceivably uneven staircase. It was a modest accommodation with a highly deceptive approach and entrance. In fact, *deceptive* would be an understatement for its portrayal. Leela could bet that most people would give up even on the idea of checking out the place just by looking at its ingress.

The room was on the third floor of a timeworn building with no elevator. Leela chose it for more reasons than one — to begin with, its proximity to her office was barely a 7-minute walk, which is considered a luxury in any city; and well, this was Bombay. Add to it, how wonderfully ventilated the room was; It had tons of natural light and air gushing in from all four sides.

Incidentally, if there was one parameter that Leela was sure of, while choosing her accommodation, it was this — *the room should be well lit*, so this place instantaneously struck a chord with her. Besides, there was a small open space right outside the room — an unattached balcony so to speak, which is again a rare sight in the city. Despite how shabbily the room was kept, she could visualise giving it a complete makeover using her creativity and converting the room into a nice cosy space.

So that's how Leela first met the lively and magnanimous Olvin Fobler, and the rest is history. In hindsight, she ascertains that the best part about that accommodation was that she was just a lane away from the Foblers'. In no time, from a stranger, he became her treasured friend and guardian. In a city as bustling and large as Bombay, where people tend to feel lonely even with their families around, Leela never felt she was alone. She knew that if she ever needed anything at all, Fobler was there to fix it for her. That's the kind of confidence he evoked in her.

Like a guardian, he watched over her to ensure she settled in well, and like a friend, he inadvertently taught her to live life to the fullest. He was extremely fond of Leela and introduced her to his folks with a lot of pride. So much so, that his affection for her went beyond his guardianship towards her so seriously that he ended up playing cupid and fixed her up with one of his 'friends'; astoundingly, he succeeded in doing so — Leela is now married to that same 'friend' of his. (And no, just in case you were wondering, 'that friend' was not 74 years old.)

Fobler transcended aspects like age, gender, religion, or basically anything trifling in his associations. He had friends across all age groups and walks of life, with them ranging from the local carpenter and bus conductor to the renowned choreographers of Bollywood, and expat pilots of Boeing 777. His social circle was so widespread that he was sometimes referred to as *The Mayor of Bandra* by his folks. Contrasting what most men and women his age would go through, there was never a dearth of people wanting to give him company.

'Hello. Hello, Leela. I am planning to take some of my friends to Wellington Club this evening. Please join us there after your office,' he would say over a call, on a random afternoon.

'Is there an occasion?'

'No, not really! Do you need an occasion to have a good time?'

'Haha… I would have loved to join, but I have a friend coming over today — if only I'd known about this plan before…'

'Oh, ok. You could get your friend along as well. It'll be fun, unless of course, your friend doesn't want to join us.' That was his magnanimity.

The man celebrated life every day. He didn't need any reason to make merry. He would host parties at his place and have his close friends over for drinks and dinner every other week, and on some occasions, he would host a select few at one of the Gymkhanas. In fact, Leela had never partied as much as she did while she was living in that neighbourhood — thanks to Olvin Fobler.

Leela enjoyed his camaraderie so much that she would often ditch plans of going out with her other friends and colleagues and choose to be in his company instead. Beholding him, one would wonder if he ever had any dull moment at all. When with him, she would forget all her worries too. She reminisces that while he was not the kind who would discuss spirituality as a subject, his way of life was quite spiritual in essence.

Olvin Fobler is no longer alive. And yet, he is as awake, alive, and kicking in Leela's memories. Although Leela always wanted to experience Bombay professionally, it was the city she saw through Fobler's eyes that she instantly fell in love with. That love for Bombay ignited by Fobler has not ceased to grow even over the years and now she calls it home too, very much like Fobler did.

Leela no longer lives in that neighbourhood, but the good times she had over there stay evermore with her all along. Just like the sea compliments and brings Bombay to life, Fobler will continue to remain an integral part of her life story.

As for Olvin Fobler, Leela proclaims him to be her coolest friend of all times and can bet that he is now chilling — most likely with a glass of whiskey in his hand — and spreading happiness in some parallel world.

So long.

14

An Indelible Phase

by Yumna Usmani

"I got your back, man!" Grover said. I don't know how to thank him in a cool, manly way, so, I give him an encouraging smile.

—Rick Riordan

Looking up from my book, I smile with a sigh.

Before I boarded the train, on the phone my mother told me about the time when I was a toddler and we had travelled to Darjeeling. Mother said that I kept running all around the train. I had even made a teenage boy my friend; he had given me a cute keyring. And I can't stop thinking about it.

I'm on the train, homeward bound, and sitting on the window-facing single-seater. Present diagonally across from me, a couple, and a father with his son who looks to be about six or seven years old. The son keeps on asking questions, hugging, jumping, and giggling on his bearded father's tummy. The father and son remind me of me and my father. I turn to the view outside and get back to my past.

I was seven my father lost his job; he sat at home for a whole year. That was when I discovered who my father was, the kind of person he was. It wasn't that we weren't friends— we were such good friends that every well-wisher of ours knew me not only as his daughter but his close friend as well. All I wanted for a happy life was my father, my books and knowing how to cook.

Now, the cooking part was for my father, because then I could whip out sweet delicacies for him and let him have as much as he wanted. That same November, dad got ill and ended-up with Diabetes. And my heart had broken up into pieces. Because only then I realised nothing lasted forever; dreams didn't always come true. All my life, no matter what I did, this proved true in every circumstance.

Thinking back to what Grover said in Rick Riordan's book, I am reminded of a person I had said something similar to.

Buried beneath books since a young age when, at the time of ripping-glue-gunk-from-hands was a game, I found a friend in another human like me. Just like a family-man who finds the perfect Christmas tree in a Christmas tree farm, I found the one I was unknowingly looking for. Our stars may have been linked though. She was the kind who could talk to multiple types of people at the same time and still get them to agree to a point. Exploring everything that the school library could provide was our favourite game.

Soon we were carrying around the borrowed books, discussing the fate of Beatrice Prior and fingering the *Inkworld* map while the rest of the school chanted the name of a sports team we couldn't care less about. We'd imagined growing up together and becoming editors, like we had a clue that one day we'd be losing each other.

She had always been smarter. Always surrounded by hordes of people, she made friends tirelessly. That taunted me away. It seemed like the worst-case scenario, which I wish it was… But it wasn't. Sometimes, it's worser than you can imagine. Unfortunately, the shenanigans of life can cause a catastrophe as infinite as that of a tornado. You choose how you'd like to look at it.

The most treasured moments of my life came from that gem I stumbled upon all those years ago. Heck! I was too young, and dumb to know her worth. Cursing Dolores Umbridge, we coursed through the years of American boy bands together. Her Mr. Holmes brain and my Mr. Mark Manson personality made a good team. But the irony of Holmes being a piece of fiction and Manson a very living, breathing human was not lost on us.

Soon, she went on in search of the Watson for her Sherlock. It all got a little uncomfortable for us both. Petty disagreements became serious issues over time. Bickering, as that of Ronald Weasley and Hermione Granger soon grew to proportions of that between Snape and McGonagall.

"I'd tell me, if I were you." I said, this one time we broke into an argument.

"Well, but you are not."

"We are ending this on *that* note? Just like that?"

"Oh! Am I supposed to give a whole concluding speech to close this… this — whatever this is?"

"*This* is an argument. And no thank you, but a 'so this is what you want, here you go' would work."

"This is not an argument."

"We have been at it, for like a whole day! What else is it, if not an argument?"

"You are frustrating."

"Sure. Say that to me and run off to those people you like to hang out with."

"They are my friends." *Then, who am I?*

She walked out of the room, leaving my in the empty hallway filled with the fresh smell of flowers and a sour mood.

Because 'one mustn't settle for less,' we kinda, sorta knew what was coming. Acceptance — it came into action; it dived headfirst into the situation. As it took over the reins of the 'friend-ship' we sailed on and lead it astray, we accepted it. We eventually saw that we couldn't stay like that forever. Wind hit me hard enough to shake my balance and the said string cut loose and we both fell apart.

Back in the present, I wonder what brought on this reverie. I think back to the times I made memories worth remembering. They help me in my anxiety, lull me to sleep on the worst of nights.

Having to join another school, I'd put on my shy-personality suit and walked right into the new crowd. To nobody's surprise, I didn't fit in. In every person I came across, I'd look for glimpses of her only to realise that the spark was gone with her; it was all history. It hit me like a wrecking ball. I realised then that I should have treasured all the things she told me. I should have carried them safely with me. I realised what I once had should have been valued. I realised the worth of the gem I held in my palm. I realised then... and I realised too late.

Too bad, I threw the gem into the ocean thinking of it as a stupid stone. Only heard the noise it made diving in, rather than the secrets it shouted at me. And now… now, it was gone with the void. The oceanic waves of the crowd swallowed her. Disheartened and distorted, I went about my day giving way too less shits about people around me and my new environment.

One fine day, stumbling through the crowds with the baggage on my shoulder, I heard a voice.

"Steady thy self!" it said. My eyes then lifted to black eyes boring into mine.

Lightly, I shot back, "It is unusually attractive to hear someone quoting *Tom Hazard* in a swarming crowd." The face made of high bones grinned.

That somebody-is-being-too-friendly-alarm went off in my head. It was not the first time I felt those; but certainly, first, in response to the person standing there. *It could become either: uncomfortable or comfortable.* Tell you what, ever since that encounter, what I felt was certainly somewhere in the between territory.

This is new... I had thought to myself; I didn't know such feelings existed. Those warning bells started going off at a dangerous rate. In the void of then, I still felt an unfamiliar spark when all of that happened. But it felt sweet, when the reason for those jitters in the pit of my stomach were some references to the fictional world where I wanted to make an igloo for myself and never ever leave it. Also, one — I was looking for a spark anyway, and two— these gave me an awful lot of comfort.

Soon, it all got too tingly-munchy and lovely. The feelings I had read about a thousand of times were now in my heart. These went on for a long time when the matter settled with us being way too good a pair of... *more than friends.* We were the partners in the multiple-berry-sweet crimes that we committed. Our idea of rebellion was to cause modest troubles like staying in the library or buying a book online that was way too expensive; anything that could draw a little bit of laughter from deep our throats, we'd do all of that.

It was much later when I stalked and stumbled upon *her.* Her writing had me know that what I was reading had come from someone I used to know all too well. *My gem*, I thought. Gathering up the scraps of courage I was left with, I made a move. I heard from her. As it turned out, Mr. Holmes had found his Watson, exactly what he was looking for. And deep down I knew, Mr. Mark Manson was with his life-partner. It wasn't too bad after all. I had someone to make sugary-sweet things for, and she had someone worthy of her.

The partner I thought I was with, did not turn out to be quite so. And let us not get into what happened when I came upfront to face the truth; the unspeakable gut-wrenching pain and everything that had ever been felt by every fictional character in the literary universe, experienced by the non-fictional humans.

In all these memories of people I have, there is also one other person to have left a huge footprint in my life. They have shown me the light to a way I am forever happy to take. This woman enlightened me in the course of self-awareness and self-grooming, with the word 'enlightenment' being one of the big, heavy words she introduced me to. She was my teacher in elementary school. I, very unfortunately, do not remember the first time we met. Also, we did not know that a lesson on a random Tuesday was the last time we were to see each other.

Of all the things I wanted to become, being a public speaker was a prominent one. She was open with us, her students. If I ever become a teacher, I want to be one like her. I desired to be her, akin to what little girls think of barbie dolls. I was bullied for having a loud laughter as a child, so much so, that I stopped laughing in the school boundaries for a good stretch of time. And then came she, who had the charm that worked on people no matter how loud her laughter or voice was. She was an iconic woman in the most un-woman-ish way. She taught me to never be afraid.

She had me re-thinking all the things I have ever perceived and register how wrong I was. I am telling you about her not for nothing. This information is intended to explain how exactly I survived all the hits and blows I narrated about earlier. She is the reason I am strong enough to date, to stand in the ashes of who I used to be and not be ashamed of it.

But the whole reason for bringing these unnerving painful stories or say 'chapters of my life' is also a painful pill to swallow.

These four or five people were once physically present in my life, now they remain in my heart. All of them are there for a significant reason — these reasons, though, are unexplainable. But if I had to put them in words, it would be in such a manner.

When I picture it, I see colours colliding. I don't know why, but they all have a colour for themselves. I see a blank canvas first, then it is covered by colours that my mind has identified for each of them; they flow from different directions, and they even meet in the middle, perhaps that's me. But one's path different then the another's and the colours in the middle do not unite. They all come to a point and stop flowing. Just like that. I think it symbolizes the irony of how one person does meet the other; they all just met me. They taught me lessons that some lucky people get to learn the easy way; I got to have it the hard way.

The best friend taught me to be open to knowledge. To seek from wherever you can and not to restrict it to a certain something.

And my father. Well, all that happened to him and all that he was, taught me to dream but not to imagine. He once explained to me, saying, "It is perfect to dream for things and not to want them. But you've got to make sure you know that you are not compelled to reach it. Because then, your mind will trick you into thinking that life will go just the way you want it to. That makes you expect… and that will leave you heartbroken."

He also said "Dream about the dragons, dream the world unseen, but never believe yourself to be fated for it; never think of being fated to anything. Welcome change whenever it comes your way. Have tea, have it with lemon, telling *change* that you've been waiting for it to come."

The partner. The lover. The lessons learned the hard way. Heartbreaks are actually worst when you have them. It's an ache in the moment, but after the fact, it teaches you not to be afraid. Of anything.

The person I am today is all shaped and moulded by these memories and people. I wonder why people don't value things when they have them. But anyways, whatever I know and am good at is all because of all these experiences. I left school and understood the thing called adapting. Met people who were complete strangers to me and learned to call them friends.

The teacher, she is the reason I am strong enough today to stand in the ashes of who I used to be and not be ashamed of it. I understood that everyone leaves a footprint. Not just a carbon footprint but something more than that. Something deeper and heavier than that.

All of a sudden, I am conscious of the noisy compartment. It was the train coming to a screeching halt, jarring me awake; I find that the train has reached my station. And this little boy on the train, perhaps my reason for diving into memories, has reminded me to look back to who I used to be and who I am now; to keep appreciating myself and walk on, being braver than ever. Another souvenir for my collection, or rather, *recollection.*

I know now why they say all the things they say. Smile loud and speak low, they say. And so, as I make my way out, I turn, giving him an encouraging smile and walk toward the exit door… hoping that, maybe, he will grow up to be a happy person. Yes, life is unfair, but for how long can it remain that way?

15

Wagging Through Life

by Yash Karmancherry

It was a lazy school-free Saturday afternoon at least for me, but my mother worked through it tirelessly. The doorbell rang. 'Go out and play, Roshni!' said mother as she opened the door for yet another of her business partners. I hated going out to play, not because I didn't like playing, which obviously, I don't think any kids my age disliked, but because going out of the house made me feel lonely — going to the run-down park in our vicinity and frolicking in the sand on my own while I saw the others ever so conveniently play as if they'd known each other their whole life wasn't my idea of fun.

'Hey girl! You want to play some catch?' asked one of them.

I responded with an awkward nod that I meant to have understood either way. They looked at me for a few seconds and then interpreted it in the manner I hoped and left me to my own devises.

I always found it difficult to initiate conversations with strangers and act like I was interested in their lives and believe that they were in mine. I couldn't put on a show to fit in like the other kids and the only person I knew inside-out was my mother, who seemed to be getting busier day by day. She was the lone human in the whole-wide-world whose life I was actually interested in. But it seemed to me, even at that young age, like we were losing the bond we had shared before. It really hurt, but I understood that the financial burden came onto my mother's shoulders after my father's demise. She had to single-handedly repay the debts of my father's medical expenses, ones that hadn't improved my father's health but only prolonged his suffering while leaving our family with monetary constraints and emotional turmoil. Back in the playground mentally, I shook-off the grief knowing there wasn't anything that could be done now, other than being understanding toward my living parent.

I felt a sudden discomfort when a sound pierced my ears, from underneath a gutter nearby. It sent chills down my spine and got me curious. I walked towards the sound and tried picking the heavy slab covering it but found no success. After all, I was only a Seven-year-old girl trying to lift a concrete block that probably weighed as much as I did. On hearing the low-pitched whining coming from below the gutter I stood next to, the group of kids playing in the garden walked towards me and tried to investigate.

'How do you make that sound?' they asked me.

Having all of their eyes on me was really uncomfortable. They waited for a response which I wasn't sure I could give, and as their wait increased, the more conscious I felt of having to say something that made sense. But how could I when I myself didn't know? So, instead I tried pulling the slab, and managed to move it a crack. The whining stopped all of a sudden and a meek bark could be heard in its place.

The bark was unsure and scared, much like what my voice would have sounded, had I tried to respond to the group of kids along with the added trouble of finding the right words. Nevertheless, it was a relief that I didn't need to answer their question as we all got busy removing the big block of concrete together. Once it came off, there lay the most lovable thing I'd ever laid my eyes upon. A cute brown puppy was lying in filth. I rushed forward and grabbed the puppy with both my arms and brought it out.

'That puppy is so adorable!' said one of the girls, peeking over the shoulder of the boy who helped me remove the slab. I looked at its eyes and it stopped whining. I felt like it understood me without my having to go through the usual formalities of acting in any manner to gain attention. At that moment, it felt like it was my opportunity to find a companion.

I held it like a baby and gazed at it. The pup was a dark chocolate kind of brown with big dark eyes. It was surely not one of those fancy fluffy-haired dog breeds or at least didn't seem like one, not with the scantiness of the hair on its body. It had a tail that moved so fast that it was nearly invisible.

'Where did you come from?' I wondered if it was he or she, and if it had a name and a home before.

And I asked that tiny face, 'Would you like a new home?' to which it made an expression that could be perceived, I assumed, as a wholehearted. *Yes, please!*

I ran home, gleefully and showed the pup to my mother, 'Look at this adorable ball — Please, please let me keep him!' My grandfatherly neighbour had mentioned it was a *he*, in passing, as I ran up the stairs. My mother was hesitant to my request since she wasn't fond of pets and didn't have time to take care of one either.

I pleaded with all my heart to keep him, but she didn't budge.

'If you want a pet so much… grow up, buy your own house and *then*, get one for yourself.' At first, I cried till the sky fell to earth but then I remembered the responsibility I had toward my mother — to be supportive.

I took the puppy back downstairs to give him some water and biscuits. 'If it were up to me, I'd treat you as family and make sure we have the best of times with each other.'

With a heavy heart, I prepared myself to bid him goodbye, but those eyes seemed to speak to me, provide courage, and assure me that everything would be alright. I didn't want to go back to feeling lonely again. I knew that I had to be obedient to my mother, but at the same time, I wasn't going to lose the opportunity of being loved and cared for.

I looked at the puppy and sighed at my inner turmoil. Beside us, there was a massive carton box which had been discarded by someone a few days before. It seemed large enough to shelter him and *that* was enough for me to interpret as a sign that he was meant to stay.

I carried him and said 'Courage' to which he barked a couple of times and spun in rapid circles, his bushy tail wagging as if to approve the name given to him.

I said, 'This is your home from today,' as I opened the box up to make sure it was in a good condition. 'I'm sorry that I can't let you stay with me. That decision isn't mine. But I am going to take care of you like you're my little brother.'

From that day on, I waited for mother to send me out as usual when she was busy. I didn't feel left out anymore. Never was there a moment that I felt my company would bore Courage.

'I really miss my father.' I felt like saying the kind of things that were stuck in my head but were never shared out loud to anyone, scared of the opinions people would have.

'You know, Courage, sometimes I think about how different life would be if he was around. My mother wouldn't have as much weight on her shoulders and perhaps I'd have someone to — *Yeww*! At least, don't lick my lips after you've just eaten. I can literally taste it!'

Eventually, my mother saw the difference that Courage was making in building me as a person and the strong bond we had built. She gave it to my continued pleas. I ran downstairs to the box and exclaimed, 'We are going to be sharing a room!' I carried him home and never again felt hesitant to express my love through hugs, pats and cuddles.

Over the next few years, Courage became an irreplaceable part of not only my life, but of our small family. The woman who was set against me getting Courage home, my mother gradually became the one closest to him. Courage managed to keep her busy and my mother got somebody to talk to while I was at school.

My mother spent hours with him, conversing about literally every little thing.

Sometimes, it was about me. 'She's growing up too soon. Don't you think so, Courage? Yes, I agree... you're growing too!'

Sometimes, it was about her everyday troubles.

'The vegetables are becoming expensive! Unaffordable!'

'The neighbours think we are a ration shop... with the number of times they keep coming to ask for groceries!'

He made sure that he gave some sort of feedback while we were ranting by rubbing his head against our legs to comfort us or by sighing every once in a while. His responses reassured us that we had his attention with the encouragement. He proved time and again that he was the best listener in the house.

Courage made me wish that all humans were as good listeners as him. His reactions were that cute — licking-up faces and feet, tilting his head to a side and looking up at us with those puppy eyes. The next few years flew by smoothly as Courage managed to fill the void that was created when my father left us.

Soon I became preoccupied with academics and as I progressed through high school. I understood my emotions and expressed them better. I began feeling confident about my identity and what I was capable of. This helped me become more social and be involved in extra-curricular activities. This new-found persona of mine kept me busy. I didn't find as much time, as I previously did, to just rant about all my problems to Courage. I felt the joy when he barked every time, I reached the colony's gate and drenched me with his saliva as soon as I entered the house. I was sorry that I couldn't spend as much time with him anymore. Even so, I was satisfied with the way life was going about.

'I can't believe that the day to move has finally come. I'll be leaving you and mother behind,' Tears were rolling down my cheeks. 'And also, this house. Courage… I really don't know how I'm going to manage. I really don't. I don't think I'll be able to sleep in a bed other than mine… *especially* without having my fluffy li'l doggo lying next to me.'

'Who or what will I cuddle with?' I asked while running my hands through Courage's fur as if it were the last time. Holding back the tears, I stated 'But…. This ought to be done. It's for a brighter future and I always wanted this.' With a heavy heart, I said my goodbyes to my mother and Courage.

I reached the college gate and felt unwelcomed by the hundreds of intimidating faces. The sense of security that I had achieved regarding my identity seemed to be at risk again. Just looking at my peers who all seemed to have come from more privileged and well-informed families threatened the entire concept of who I believed I was. It led to sleepless nights of questioning if I belonged there, among those people.

Heading to lectures and passing by my peers reminded me of an all-too-familiar feeling that hadn't been experienced, for ages. Entering the class was the most difficult part of the day. It was a stressful, the experience of walking through the entire room and the glances from either side — benches with students who seemed to have already developed cordial relations with each other. It made me feel like I joined the institute a couple of years after everyone else did and, hence, I missed out on discovering people of my liking or kind earlier.

All of them were now taken or already part of groups I didn't feel privy to. The conversations that I heard others having were gibberish to me. Neither did I relate to them, nor did I feel like relating. It seemed like a difficult five months in the hostel, and I was glad that I was finally homeward bound.

Going home meant eating the kind of food which, as soon as it caressed my taste buds, shot a hundred memories of occasions I savoured similar meals on the very intimate dining table. Also, the conversations, activities, and experiences associated with that taste. But mostly, going home also meant falling asleep with Courage wrapped in my arms and waking up to him licking my face. I was keen to be reminded that I belonged somewhere.

There is a certain sense of safety that one experiences when they come within a walkable distance of home. Seeing familiar faces and places simultaneously after such a distance in space and time made me feel the comfort already. As soon as my cab halted, I could hear the bark. It was the sound that I had longed to hear every night I forced myself to sleep as I lay in my loneliness.

Courage came running and pounced on me. 'Did you miss me, boy?' I asked, to which he responded with a happy *Woof.* 'Good boy, Courage!' I played with his ears and looked him in the eye, instantly feeling the flame re-ignite. I found my identity again just by holding him in my arms and the knowledge of being truly loved returned full force.

To no surprise, I was greeted with the same broad smile and warm hug from my mother that I had received during my entire childhood, every day, as I returned from school. Walking into my house and breathing in its nostalgic setting was the final missing piece in restoring my identity and confidence.

I returned for the next term a month later, reborn. I had found myself again and didn't need another person's approval because I knew who I was inside. I flourished in college since then and never again second-guessed myself. Courage stayed true to his name and provided me with a push every time I thought I had no chance of getting back up. He proved to be the one of the most, if not the most, humane characters in my life.

16

The Teacher

by James Bowers

In my not-so-long-ago youth, at the age of sixteen, I thought I was the smartest person in the room; even when among teachers. I was intelligent, but I had a hard time channelizing it. My attitude wasn't the best either; instead of striving for more, I chose not to work and turn in assignments, as if to say—*I'm too smart to try.* I think, all this was a reflection of what I was dealing with at home. See, at the time my mom had been diagnosed with breast cancer. To say the least, my family was struggling— and the feeling followed me to school as well.

I didn't care about my schooling, and I definitely didn't care about the adults around me. I felt that I had much bigger things going on personally, than learning or homework. I have two brothers— both older, and both were dealing with my mom's illness in different ways. Even though we had one another, none of us were able to support the other two. This entire event felt like it drifted us away to different islands where we were forced to deal with everything on our own. We were devastated by our situation, but in ways I didn't see coming, it would change us; for me in particular, it would lead to the place where I'd meet the man that would change not only my life, but my entire perspective on how I viewed the world.

Eventually, my lack of concern for graduating caught up with me and I was given a few options by the school dean, a guidance counselor, and a few teachers that seemed to care. They suggested that I get my G.E.D. or be held back plus summer and Saturday school, or maybe a continuation school. One of my brothers had already got his G.E.D., so, that seemed feasible.

Though I chose it for one reason or another, continuation school turned out to be one of the best decisions I've ever made. My mom had to come and enroll me before I could start taking classes. But for her, finding time and strength to do so was difficult since she was doing her chemotherapy at the time. Luckily, all she had to do was sign some papers and meet the principal.

On the day of enrollment, I had to do a quick interview with the principal. He immediately insisted that I had been smoking weed and arrived high. We went back and forth, "No I don't smoke weed sir, never have."

"Are you sure, Mr. Alvarez? Your eyes say otherwise."

"Believe me, Sir. I'm just tired... really. I don't smoke weed."

"Well, let's bring your mother in here. Maybe, she can weigh in on this." He made me take a math test and an English test while my mother sat in and watched. The test was to gauge where my skill level was — but the majority of the interview was just him asking if I smoked weed, which was very annoying. A week went by, and it was finally time to start my first day of class.

The school was small— the entirety of it was within four tiny buildings. There was one math teacher who also taught chemistry, and a social-studies teacher who taught everything, from economics to volleyball, including English which was my first class. I walked into the classroom and made a direct shot for the back of the room. I was applying my time-tested strategy of *head down, ears up and they'll leave me alone;* although, that only worked when the teacher didn't care.

The teacher introduced himself to the class, to the new students, "I'm Bartholomew Warburton, but you all can call me *Mr. W.*" He had this strange vibe; the energy that came off of him seemed soft and caring. The class looked excited and ready to learn, at the same time they were worried — to find out what he had planned. But they all looked glad to be there and he had their attention before the lesson had begun.

Mr. W was the center of attention in a room full of teenagers who didn't like school. He was dressed unprofessionally, less than formal for sure, almost like a relaxed, laid-back, and sitting in the park while the sun shines and music is playing style. The hour began and he placed a picture on the whiteboard in front of us. He turned to the class and asked what we saw. The other kids gave answers that he immediately shot down if wrong. "It's a witch on her broom!" "NO!"

"Oh... Oh, maybe a wave of water." "No!"

Finally, he called on me, "Hey you, in the back with the head down— the new guy trying to hide so no one calls on him, yeah you! Tell us what you think." He was laughing and chuckling through his teeth the whole time he said that.

I raised my head— stared at the picture for a few seconds to give the illusion that I was thinking— and then answered. "Pictures and paintings can mean a thousand words, maybe that's what we're looking at." My classmates all murmured under their breaths — *Of course, thought-provoking words were just spoken.* I wasn't right, but I wasn't wrong. My goal was to just sound smart enough to be left alone.

Mr. W looked impressed for a few seconds, even speechless... until he wasn't. "No, that's wrong as well." He spun the picture right-side up and said, "It was just upside down— ahahahhah!"

As he laughed, some students let out a cry of familiar frustration. It seemed as if this happened often in his class. He walked over to me and paused for a second, "Let me guess, you're smart, but you like to be left alone. So, you put your head down, say something astute, and hope they leave you alone, right? Well. Sorry, kid. That's not gonna happen here. You're gonna have to participate if you wanna pass... my class." He had me— I was shocked, which was impressive because at this point in my life no adult had done that to me before. It was becoming clear that this school or this classroom wasn't going to go the way I thought it would.

As the year unfolded, Mr. W taught me many things about myself, about life, and about the world— which was strange to me back then as he didn't look like the type of person that had such insights. He always wore a long muscle shirt draped by a flannel. He had long grey hair that flowed down to his back and he rocked a grey beard. Though he was up in age, he carried himself with energy and pep, excited for the day. It seemed like he didn't have a care in the world like his shoulders had never felt the weight of it, which wasn't the case, as I found out — over time, he just learned to let go of the stress, and pressures of the world.

He liked to use a particular phrase when it came to explaining why and how he came upon this behavior. "You can't break the rules until you learn them first. You see, like this essay for example— which you have to know how to build and what goes where— it needs specific structure, a topic sentence and a conclusion; and where does the climax fit in? Once you know all those rules, you can start to break them, and you can add *your* unique spin on the story." A simple take on life, that I found myself applying to life in and outside of school.

Mr. W taught me that intelligence accursed one to be curious and we all know what curiosity did to the cat. He pulled me aside one day and we had a talk during lunch. "You don't look so good, Brandon. Is something wrong?" "No, I'm ok."

"That's what everyone says when they're hiding what's wrong. There's no harm in talking." "Ok, but... it's just that sometimes I don't feel like life is worth it… *At times.*"

"Well, that's definitely a big deal, but a natural thought. I was in the habit of thinking like that, too. I used to feel that there wasn't much of a good reason to keep going." "You're still here though… so, what made you change your mind?"

"Being smart is a wonderful thing, but it can be a curse as well. See, you're self-aware and can think beyond yourself; you can ponder and wonder about life and death and think about what's to come— which can be scary. But we can't control that part of life, we can only control what's in front of us— in the moment. Not what *will be.*"

"I guess that never occurred to me. I've always let my thoughts run wild… until I'm drowning in them."

"The human mind can be a dangerous place, especially when you're smart and a teenager with unsure thoughts on the world and yourself." He wasn't trying to scare me but warn me; warn me about the dangers of depression and self-loathing that come with the ability to have self-awareness, and the fear and questions they can stir up.

Mr. W was showing us another way to live this life — to make it a less dreadful version where we complain less and take up on the world and its opportunities. He encouraged us to live a life worth living, no matter what we chose for a career. His job was to teach students so they might leave the school with a semblance of education— but he did better than that. He got a classroom of teens to yearn for more out of life than just money and success.

He showed us that passion and love were more important than any amount of wealth. Don't get me wrong, his head may have been in the clouds, but his feet were firmly planted on the ground. He understood that we lived in the real world and money made it go round. He kept us grounded in that regard; he made sure we made goals we could keep and achieve, but that we still dreamt big. "Listen, money isn't everything. But it's important since it's a part of the world we live in. Choose your jobs and careers wisely, don't just take the highest paying gig because it pays the most; you can have all the riches in the world and still be miserable. If you follow your dreams, money is sure to follow, of course, as long as you're putting in the effort." That school was a small stop in my life that didn't last long, but it changed me completely.

These people that come into our lives are sent to us like guiding spirits embodied through fate to show us the way. It's up to us to take notice, apply, and learn the teachings they bring us even when their own lives might not be perfect. Some of us get more chances than others because we might need them— just like that institution, where no student was alike; each needed a different method of learning; and the teachers we had, knew this.

The school wasn't perfect, but perfect wasn't what we required. We just needed some hope and guidance, for once in our lives—for someone to say, "You can do it! Believe in yourself, even when you fail." It wasn't a cure-all situation, either. I saw kids drop out and give up, but they didn't just become a hollowed memory of an empty chair— there was a person in that seat; the teachers and students, all cared when they stopped showing up. They would ask, "Do you know where he is? Well, call his phone and tell him I said to get his butt in class."

The school became a safe space to experience oneself in a controlled environment. Ideas weren't shot down but persuaded to explore; there was free roam with the right amount of discipline for the ones who wanted to learn. No one was bad at learning, no one was stupid; learning was a skill that needed to be honed and sharpened. Mr. W gave us a chance to get better without the fear of not being good enough. He was hard at times and soft at others— for those that needed it. No one ever felt hated or attacked, from what I gathered and understood.

Eventually, the teachers that mattered left. Some retired within the year I attended, this included Mr. W; some got better jobs, but you can't blame them— they had dreams and aspirations that they still wanted to achieve. I never hated them for leaving, even though the next group of teachers that came were, clearly, more interested in their pay checks than the needs and wants of their students.

Before Mr. W left, he said his goodbyes to everyone. "Today is our last day, and even though I won't be your teacher anymore, I hope you all still remember the things we've learned together. Your lives are about to change just as mine is; but that doesn't mean we should be scared. Change is a mystery, but not something to fear. It is inevitable and you can't always control when it arrives or how it presents itself. All we can do is stand tall and do our best to handle what comes our way."

I've changed a lot since then and for the better, of course. And that's the beauty of it all; we're not meant to stay the same. Change is imminent — we must adapt and move right along with it. Time doesn't stop moving. Neither should we.

PART 5

// WHO ARE YOU? //

Mirrors of all shapes and sizes

17

Diaspora

by Sharad Narayan

Strangers at Vidyarthi Bhavan

Some chance encounters leave lasting impressions on us — they make us take stock of who we are, inspire us to do things, and perhaps even prod us to be better humans. This was one such encounter; and it marked the beginning of my journey as a writer.

The year was 2016 and it was festive season in late October. This usually meant, depending on the vagaries of the Lunar calendar, either Navaratri or Deepavali. That year, it was the latter. As is expected with Deepavali, it brought with it the annual urge to binge-shop for clothes. Since our celebrations generally aren't lavish, I decided to take my mum out shopping to *Desi*. She hadn't been there ever, so I knew she would enjoy herself.

On the designated day, I wound up work and proceeded to the under-construction R. V. Road metro station at 3:15 pm. The understanding was that we'd rendezvous there and go to the *Desi* store at Seetha Circle. Some minor confusion later, where we ended up on opposite exits of the station (thanks B.M.R.C.L), we were on our way. As I predicted, mum enjoyed herself; an apt metaphor to this would be 'akin to a kid in a candy store.' An hour later, at 5 in the evening, we left there with happy hearts and lighter wallets. Since we were in the vicinity of the place and it was on the route home, I suggested an evening snack at *Vidyarthi Bhavan*, to which she readily agreed.

For the uninitiated, Vidyarthi Bhavan is a famous eating joint situated in the heart of Basavanagudi, Bangalore. One of the oldest eateries in town, this is still holding its own in the midst of *McDonald's, KFC*, and other nearby forms of coronary embolism. It has lost a lot of its old class, though; what remains is homage to a fading legacy. However, the charm is never lost; more than one patron will swear to have 'been there when DVG was dining at the table across him.' A certifiable wonder of the world must be the waiters here, who must have been circus artistes, given the ease with which they balance 20 plates, laden with *dosais*, in 2 hands.

Going through the customary wait of getting a seat, we eventually made our way to the back of the seating area. Across us was an elderly couple; retirees it seemed, who were still buying into the 'pensioner's paradise' hoax. We sat and placed our orders; a *masala dosai* and a v*ada* each, for both of us.

As we tried to make ourselves as comfortable as possible on the cramped wooden bench, I noticed something very odd with the couple from earlier; the lady leaned onto the man rather awkwardly, in what could be misinterpreted as a display of affection. My first thought was *that's so quaint; she's keeping romance alive.* A second later the thought evaporated; *elderly lady, prim and proper, dressed in a lovely saree, overtly showing affection?* Something seemed amiss. Surely enough, it was; next moment, she leaned her head back. I noticed that the right side of her face had become slack as she leaned, and her eyes were starting to roll backwards. I immediately registered that she was having a cardiac incident. It was at least a year after this that I learnt the F.A.S.T. acronym and its utility in identifying stroke victims.

The husband was initially unperturbed, pretending nothing was really wrong. He attempted to feed her some sugar and wash it down with water. This was futile, as her facial musculature had become extremely weak. By this time, several people were alerted to the situation and had started raising a furore on what needed to be done. It spoke volumes about the degree of imperviousness that the crowd of people were accustomed to — that they weren't able to identify the gravity of the situation — still intent on feeding her salt and pickle to rennervate her. All through this, the husband was insisting that his wife was completely normal. He kept patting her cheek, thinking she was going to shake out of her torpor and sit upright again.

At that moment, right as it seemed like the situation would devolve completely, a doctor appeared out of the crowd of diners. She, with the patience of a Buddhist monk, convinced the man that it was necessary to shift his wife right away to the hospital. As the husband ambled away, she went on to perform basic checks: the woman's pulse, her pupil movement, and the like. Finally, the husband reached the entrance in their car, and the lady was assisted out by several patrons. Within a few moments, he had driven out of sight, the car consumed by the voluminous traffic in Gandhi Bazaar.

As we returned to our seats, I asked the doctor if I was right in thinking it was a cardiac event. She nodded and mouthed, 'Stroke. Her pulse was erratic, and she had become cold.' She acknowledged that identifying someone having a cardiac incident immediately can save valuable time. I nodded, quite speechless from the sequence of events, and turned back to my untouched *Dosai.* As I was halfway through polishing off my order, I felt a tap on my shoulder. It was the good doctor, on her way out. She said thank you to me (for what, I don't know.) I thanked her too and watched as her retreating back disappeared among the tide of people streaming in — just another face in the crowd.

I have not seen her since. I don't even remember her face. But I cannot forget her approach to the entire situation. Personifying calmness, she was able to do her duty, helping at a time of crisis, amidst a crowd of quacks and stamping her authority on what needed to be done. At the same time, I cannot seem to forgive the husband and his blasé attitude to an unexpected problem. No doubt there are brownie points for calling your wife normal in public — but pray forebear, especially at the time of a crisis? Mansplaining in such situations is something all husbands are guilty of. It speaks volumes of how patriarchal we are as a society, and how far we must go before treating all sexes as equal and worthy of respect.

Who Are You?

> "I woke up in a Soho doorway, a policeman knew my name;
> He said 'You can go sleep at home tonight if you can get up and walk away'..." — Pete Townshend, 1978

In June 2019, I was scheduled to meet a student of mine on a Sunday at *Coffee House*. The plan was for us to discuss how he should be taking his thesis forward. Needless to say, a visit to Church Street always offers up opportunities to make a *Blossoms* raid. I decided to go to the new *Blossoms* this time; dollops of nostalgia aside, the old *Blossoms* can get really crowded and claustrophobic, and I wasn't in a mood for that.

Once I entered, I took a customary first glance at all the shelves closest to the counter. Surprisingly, the establishment seemed to have branched out into other goods of significant value; I saw an aisle dedicated to stationery and board games. It seemed like the old *Gangarams* effect had taken root, offering a one-stop shop for all academic, artistic, and time-pass pursuits; though not nearly as extensive or effective. Pulling myself out of that aisle, I picked up my shopping basket and commenced my exploration.

I proceeded towards the larger centre tables with a plethora of books, hoping something that would catch my eye. I wasn't looking for any one particular book, so I was randomly surfing the titles. At this point, I remember that I was trying to explore some of the works of Nirad C. Chaudhuri. (The backstory for this attempt at exploration was that a colleague at work had given me a decades-old copy of *The Continent of Circe*. I had read through the initial chapters of the book to be intrigued enough to explore the author further.)

Almost telepathically, a store helper asked me if I was looking for something. I mentioned the author, upon which he checked Google to see if he remembered the titles. Don't ask me why, but it seemed less like checking store inventory and more like a live-action game of Mahjong Tiles. After this 'mini memory game' he proceeded to grope around a set of shelves aimlessly, before calling out to someone who seemed to be the store manager.

This gentleman was in the midst of assisting another customer, and his ears pricked up when he heard I was looking for Nirad Chaudhuri. The customer who he was assisting just incidentally happened to be Bengali. Both of them went on to tell me how Chaudhuri was an astute observer of contemporary life during pre-Independence India, but desperately shallow in his understanding of Indian history. I had gathered as much, given that Chaudhuri subscribed to the version of the Aryan Invasion. I sensed a hint of dislike in their descriptions of his works, given that he was a staunch sympathiser of *the Raj*.

As if to emphasise how important it was and to be served a dose of nationalism, the manager offered me a book, *His Majesty's Opponent* which seemed designed to beat the drums of patriotism into my heart. Taking the book, I hastily bade them a good day and moved on.

I finished rummaging through the entire bookstore and eventually managed to pick out 4 books. Pleased with my haul, I started to move towards the billing desk, when I was caught behind several people dawdling about one of the centre tables, which was stacked with Sudha Murthy's books. One of these people in front of me took a long look at one of her books and asked her friend, 'Isn't she the one married to that... who's that guy *yaar, jo computer aur software banata hai?*' ('Isn't she the one married to that... who's that guy *dude*, computer-and-software-developing one?)

Now, on a personal note, I would like to say this youngster is far more admirable than some of the other clueless numpties we are forced to encounter on a daily basis. She was in a bookstore, looking at a book, and asking a question about the author — all admirable and fast-disappearing traits. On a note of generalisation, however, her question shattered some of my inner certainty.

These are millennials; kids who were born and raised in an environment where computers played a key role. How could someone from a world like this be unaware of Sudha Murthy, I wondered. Was it not obvious that she was part of the era that changed computer engineering for posterity? I recollect several articles where she was said to have sent the then-chairman of the TATA group, J.R.D. Tata, a strong-worded letter about a hiring policy that excluded women, eventually resulting in her becoming the first ever female engineer to be hired by TELCO. Her contributions to society through the work of the Infosys foundation are many.

So how does someone like this pass under the radar for the modern millennial or the staunchest feminist?

Shaking myself out of the reverie, I finally completed my billing and left. As I walked back down Church Street, I seemed to get some answers to my own questions. People do seem to pay significantly more attention to someone who's flashy, garish and comes in making a right old din, rather than someone who's subtle. It isn't entirely their fault. We have traditionally been the kind of people who think the peacock looks so much better than the roller, the barbet or the hoopoe. So, it isn't really surprising for us to hear people wax eloquent about

<insert_overhyped_mainstream_influencer>,

while looking phased out when asked about

<insert_subtle_influencer>

Such is life, I mused, and echoes of a song by *The Who* played in my head as I got home.

Matters Closer to Home

A part of life in India is the pageantry that accompanies festivals. It doesn't help matters that I was born into a *Brahmin* family; customs and traditions become so much more sacrosanct. Granted, they have their significance, but in the rush to do these things 'right,' this significance is forgotten. Having faced this 'don't ask questions, just do as I say' directive long enough, I have rejected religion. I figured, we have enough real boogeymen to face without fabricating invisible ones for ourselves.

As atheist as I am, my mother's spiritual rediscovery was a source of deep discomfort to me. Over the past few years, I have been taking up a monthly ritual, the *Amavasai Tharpanam*, with special offerings on the days when the solstice reverses. For these rituals, I was going to a *vadhyar* (Hindu priest) who stays close to my place. This was until the pandemic hit and we were confined to our houses.

The man is the personification of every form of Brahminical patriarchy and superiority that has ever been conceived. He remains, however, blissfully unaware of the fact and ploughs on with his warped world view, with several *Iyer mamas* (old men of the community)/cronies parroting him. He also takes it upon himself to parade unmarried people to all these Iyer mamas so that they may help the unencumbered souls get an ideal bride or groom. In itself, this behaviour seems like networking and trying to be helpful. When done multiple times over, it is a short skip and step away from being regarded as pimping.

Coming back to the day in question, it began with a quick shower after the morning coffee. I left to the *vadhyar's* house, praying for quick completion of the ritual, unimpeded by Iyer mamas. I got there, to find there were two people ahead of me, a regular, and another new person, looking quite downcast. Hoping to avoid chit-chat with the regular, I chose to sit apart from the group, remaining within earshot, however. This allowed me to observe the newcomer. About 35, a long face with bags under the eyes, a week-old stubble, and long straight hair till his shoulders, which he'd pulled back with a steel hairband. At his age, the hairband was merely a matter of questionable fashion choice. The vadhyar, however, thought otherwise.

Spotting the hairband, he admonished the newbie, telling him to immediately remove it, stating, 'Only women wear such things.' Just as I thought he could not double down on the obnoxious scale, he proceeded to declare, 'Those Nepalis you see around here, they have such hairstyles. They are Shudhras, and it is OK for them; you are a 'Brahmanan' and should have short hair.' (*Shudhra*: lower-caste; *Brahmanan*: upper-caste-man)

I sat there, aghast at the flippant way an entire race was addressed as a group of Shudhras. Here was a man, comfortable in his own warped worldview, nestled in his cocoon, so self-absorbed and ignorant that he did not bat an eyelid before denigrating a regional community in its entirety. (A fun fact is that Brahmins are the 2nd largest ethnic group in Nepal, with the Yadavs, the upper-castes' favourite doormat, forming only 4% of the population)

In retrospect, it is amply clear that this is a systemic problem. Racial bias and stereotyping have normalised to such an extent, that the people who face it end up believing that to be their worth. The man who should be demonised here is merely a puppet, a product of a deeply rotten society which has trundled on for many centuries, perpetuating oppression on communities they believe to be inferior.

I left soon after, having hardly spoken to the vadhyar during the ritual. Perhaps it was my upbringing or an intrinsic value system I believed in, but I stopped myself from being harsh to him, muttering under my breath, 'Respect the age, if not anything else.' I gave him the fee for the ritual and left, having picked up plantain leaves for the lunch, on the way home. As I entered the apartment, I spotted the complex's security guy, a Nepalese Bohora man, saluting me. I smiled to myself, wondering if he had saluted because he actually respected me or simply believed in my 'superior race.'

Ah, well…

18

The Shell Boy

by Sree Yelamanchi

On a breezy evening, feet crunching in the glistening sand soaking up the perching sunrays, with ears hooked to the whispers of wintry wind and eyes gliding by the fleeting white clouds which were curtaining the silky cerulean sky, I sat lost by the shore, revelling in the earthy cologne with a tinge of salty whiff. The astral blue sea, stretching far out, was kindling its own melody echoing from the rocky cliff. And the horizon was hemmed with a silver thread. The crashing waves hissed mightily, heaping up and rolling onto the drenching sand under the grating cry of a gull; like antique witchcraft.

I unfurled my crafty brown journal, cradling in the sea hum and pining to pen away the sundown. It was a barren day when meaning to life felt bleak, purpose strayed, and spirit worn. Curling up my feet, while the briny air tickled the nostrils, I fiddled with the pen. Within my aching chest, every corner of my heart was ripping; craving for his caress like the streaming light that grazed and bleached the waters through the cloud crevices. The blanket of teal velvet exhaled onto the shell-laden wharf; the wilted seaweed seemed livelier than my botched soul. The ebbing waves barely soothed the anguish of withered dreams and butchered promises.

As my fingers cuddled the ink-bleeding quill, I gazed upon a bunch of squeaky kids immersed in framing sandcastles. My eyes ceased on a little boy with curly brown hair. He was trudging away from the lot and walking towards the turning tides. The cold current whipped up.

The boy stopped inches away from the foaming sea kissing the sands, kneeled with a twig in his hand and tardily inscribed on the wet bank. He reached into his pocket and drew out a beautiful coral flower which he carefully laid down, next to his handiwork. He stood up, sidled back, and gazed deeply as the grey tide gulped it all. He smiled and swung away from the retreating sea. He sprinted back to his friends and, shortly, the group pranced as a fierce wave washed down their crafted creations. They skipped and leaped in my direction, heedless to the castles' fate. I peered at them as they bolted past me.

The little boy braked near me. 'Are you a doctor?' he enquired; his rapt eyes glued to my knapsack.

I looked at the peeping white overcoat and back at him. 'Yes,' I nodded meekly.

'My sister wants to be a doctor when she grows up,' his eyes lit, 'She reads a lot.'

'Great! And what do you wish to be?' I asked, glancing at his lapping toes.

'I am going to be a fisherman like my father and brother,' his eyes sparkled brighter. Drowning in his deep black irises and untainted smile, I sat up, leaned in, and listened keenly. Donning a halo and dribbling warmth with a fervour so profound, he locked eyes with me. His ebony hair ruffled in the misty air.

Our sealed stares freed, when a woman in a ragged orange saree appeared in front of us, grasping a wooden cane with stacked pink candy. His smile broadened at the sight of the rose bundles. She promptly handed one to me while securing the bills I paid, in a cloth pouch. He timidly reached for the candy bag in my outstretched hand.

I watched him quickly tucking it away with a smile unfettered. 'I will take it home to my mother,' he said, clearly delighted. The sea swelled with his ardour.

'Here, take this to your mother,' I gestured to the lady for another one. Clamping the plastic bags in his palms, he looked at me with a gleam in his eyes. He briskly sat facing me, heels buried in the sand, and his tender hands snagged at the wrapping.

'Where do you live?' I asked, to which he pointed at a streak of dim flickering lights to the far north of the beach where smoke smeared the sky.

'My mother sells fish in the market,' he answered with eyes hooked on the pink cottony floss.

'Do you come here every day?' I continued, watching as he pinched a mouthful and popped it into his mouth.

'We play here every evening — and see what I found today!' he gingerly pulled out a pearly mollusc shell.

'Aliya found a bigger one!' Momentarily, his face fell as he turned towards his sprightly gang.

'It is beautiful,' I gently stroked the shell. He looked up, with glimmer cruising back in the eyes and a smile widening the corners of his mouth. The sea bellowed loudly, and my eyes followed a man tugging a boat to anchor.

'We are getting a boat—' his excited declaration brought me back, with his inoculable smile spreading onto my face, '—next month! My mother sells more fish these days.'

'My brother bought me a blue shirt yesterday,' he continued while I eyed the amulet dangling around his neck. 'He also bought my mother a saree, and a dress for my sister — both pink,' he spilled in one breath.

'And for your father?' I asked, as his toes halted toying with the sand. He hung his head low, and his black eyes deepened, 'He is not with us... he lives with the Sea God.'

My chest sharply clasped, and our smiles faded. 'The Sea God likes him a lot, so... last year... he took him and our boat.' Gloom crept into his eyes.

The knots in my stomach fastened as I gaped at him, while he slowly resumed fidgeting with his feet. I shuddered at the vision of the white fang fury of the squall dousing over the ship and sending it to copper-bottomed depths. He picked a fistful of sand and let it stream slowly between his fingers. I sat there in silence, with a throbbing heart. The only ones blaring in the lull were the growling sea and raving gust.

'Do you have school work too?' he broke the hush while plucking at the swaying hand-sewn bookmark that dropped out of my journal, and my smile steadily revisited.

'No, I just like to write...' I fumbled with the pen, 'like how you love collecting shells.' We both shared a quick look at the silvery seashell clutched in his palm.

'What do you write?' His query sent me promptly into the intimately grim spiral. I choked as the wreckage flashed in my head and the ropes of treachery strangled my voice. I struggled to articulate the tornado spinning in my heart. He looked up, drawing his knees against his chest.

'You look sad,' he paused, '...you should write there,' he gestured towards the sands he scribbled on earlier. My head swiftly sprung to decipher what he was saying but was resisted by my worn-out heart which wasn't yet ready to calm the swirl.

'I write there whenever I wish to talk to my father; my mother says the Sea God will deliver my message to him,' with his arms swinging, mirroring the waves. 'Today is his birthday, so I sent him a flower too.' His eyes were locked on the buzzing sea. My frazzled heart throbbed, and my eyes ripped.

With a dry throat, I turned to look at the western sky painted in crimson, and brushed off my wet cheeks. My heart bowed before his unblemished faith and virtue. His agony, deeper than the dark abyss, was ravaged by his pristine belief and reliance.

I ached to be him, just for a day, even for a mere minute. I spun back to him, as he shook the arm resting on my curled-up knees. 'The Sea God will fix all your troubles — he is good! See, he is sending us a boat I asked for,' a smile rounded his lips.

'I will ask my father tomorrow to talk to *Him* for you,' his arm still resting on mine. My eyes fizzled, and the vigour to hide it tattered away. All efforts to respond succumbed, under the weight of my leaden soul. I held his hand tightly, unmindful of my blurred eyes and flowing tears. His other hand reached mine, tenderly stroking it, and he gazed at me earnestly.

In a moment, he stood up, walked a little farther, and ran his fingers through the sand. He leapt back with a dried withy in his hand; forcing it in mine, he said, 'Here, write.'

My lips bore the semblance of a smile and I mumbled, 'Thank you.'

He beamed, unaware of the enormity of gratitude my heart brimmed with. We unlocked our stares as a yell echoed, 'Arul!'

A girl from the pack signalled him to join them, while a few of them dashed towards the fence on the way out. I was led astray again by how beautiful his name was, *Arul* — blessings of God. He hastily flagged back, to wait, and turned to me.

'Write before the sun goes down— the God can't read well in the dark,' he said sternly, picking up his candy.

'I will,' I chortled, softly wiping my face dry. He waved bye as he hurried towards the group, and I pulled him back by his arm.

'Take it for your sister,' I passed him my white overcoat, in a desperate attempt to ease a bit of the burden of indebtedness. He grinned ear to ear as he squeezed it to his chest. I watched him hopping away — suddenly, he stopped and rushed back. Hurriedly reaching into his pocket, he shoved the ivory shell into my hand. He dashed away, screaming and waving, 'BYE!'

I sat there pleasantly dazed and studying the shell which was partly veiled in moss. I chuckled to myself thinking how he scaled up my debt, and my eyes frantically hunted for one last glimpse of him. There he was, nearing the gate and flocked by his mates, giggling, with arms clenched around the white bundle. I lost him abruptly, as they turned direction after crossing the gate.

Far out, the hollow howl of the tides echoed, and I delicately secured the shell in a deep pocket of my bag. I stood up, dusted off myself, toted the bag onto my shoulder, and gripped the sprig in my hand. I strode onto the damp sand, and halted yards away from the crawling waves.

Kneeling under the tangerine sky I scrawled away my misery, word after word, on the wharf; along with the myriad footprints, until the golden disc receded into the turquoise waters. Just like he said. I wheeled around, basking in the mellow orange rays; the tide roared, ferrying my woes to the sea god. Clutching my bag, I plodded away — sensing the treasure inside that was assuaging my bleeding heart— and never looked back.

19

Minerva

by Pritha Samanta

It was that time of the year again. The time when the world didn't quite know what was happening. The leaves had surrendered to the inevitable process of ageing, as though giving up after a hard year. The streets had now turned auburn and crackled with every step.

In a small house on North 42nd Street in downtown Seattle, lived a teenage boy with his parents. Even though the house had enough rooms, Drie preferred the attic. Tonight, like most nights, he had decided to indulge his melancholia and had been holed up in his room. Most would agree that he was a quiet child. He was not very expressive, yet his soul was bare naked in his paintings. He used vibrant colours and created beautifully layered artwork that, unfortunately, most people did not understand.

The big black eyes stared back at him from his painting, glimmering with sorrow. This was the only distinguishable part in his otherwise abstract work. He added a tinge of gold to complete the look of innocent curiosity, mixed with hope. He took a few steps back and admired his effort. It looked so familiar. He put down his brushes and began to search for his pencils under a pile of painting rags.

"Drie!", came a voice from downstairs. It was the much-dreaded call for dinner. Sighing, Adrian Peters dragged himself away from his canvas and walked towards the narrow spiral staircase in the middle of the attic. He slowly descended the steps, not really looking forward to the prying questions from his mother about his activities and whereabouts. But as he inched closer, he could hear a murmur with a tensed tone. He entered the dining room and came to a stop.

The large room was filled with gloom. The once brightly lit trophies and mementoes lay in the shadow, next to the shaded crockery cabinet. As he scanned the unfamiliarity of the room, his eyes landed on his mother, who was seated alone at the empty table, a look of shock and despair on her face. Standing behind her, his aunt also appeared much softer; it seemed that an expression of sadness outstripped her otherwise stern features. A ball formed in the pit of Drie's stomach. He searched between his mom to his aunt, looking for an answer in their expressions. "Come, Drie. Have a seat," said his aunt in a forcefully steadied voice.

"What's the matter?" Drie asked, his voice shaking, and his eyes darting from his mom to his aunt and back to his mom. He walked towards the table and slid into a chair, all the while examining their faces. His aunt looked at his mother's gaunt face, then at Drie, and in a low whisper, murmured, "Your father is no more, Drie. We got a call from his office. He collapsed in a meeting. They rushed him to the hospital, but… couldn't save him."

Drie's mind was blank. Even in his wildest dreams, he could not have imagined what he had just heard. His father, the epitome of health and strength — the man who prided himself for having faced a few difficult situations in life, a fighter who lived through all of them with a smile and a strong mind — was no more? A low ringing sound, emanating from the middle of his head, grew stronger and stronger. Drie couldn't move. He started breathing rapidly. The ringing sound kept growing, until it was all he could hear. A numbness engulfed him while he sat there, still and staring into the dark nothingness.

***

The light crunching and crumpling continued under his footsteps. There was an air of urgency as Drie ran along the forest. The moonlight shone through the thicket and lit up a few feet ahead of him. He made his way through the woods. He ran along the trail like it was a second home to him. He could hear the water rushing in the stream below and made his way to the divergence. He paused, anxious to decide. He glanced over his shoulder for a quick second, chose a path and kept running. The blanket of leaves grew thicker under his feet. The path widened, and soon he found himself at a clearing.

Tall, mighty oak trees stared down at him. He stopped in his tracks, no longer worried about what was behind him. The soft bed of leaves on the forest floor diffused the slivers of the moonlight, only bouncing off the knobby branches. The mellow light made everything calm and slowed the pace of Drie's heart. Drie took in the beauty that was in front of him. His mood seemed to lighten, his heart now beating at a much more normal pace. The cool breeze gently caressed his long hair and calmed him.

Just as he was getting comfortable with his new reality, something moved abruptly in the clearing. Drie took in a sharp breath and turned his head towards the sound. There seemed to be some sort of creature under the leaves. He jumped behind one of the trees, drew out his head slightly, looking at the emerging figure before him.

The leaves moved and rustled, and the creature slowly lifted her head and shook-off the leaves from over her. It was a tiny little owl. She got up, wobbled lightly on her feet, while flapping her wings for balance. It was a short brown bird, with a white face. She slowly turned on her feet, still trying to steady herself. She lifted her head, and a pair of big black eyes stared straight at Drie. Drie's heart stopped. He recognized the eyes so well. The gold specs in it clearly visible in the moonlight. He swallowed hard. He was frozen to the spot. He stared back at the owl, waiting for her to move.

The owl tilted her head towards the left, still watching him. "Why are you hiding from me, Drie?" She hooted in a low deep voice.

Drie unfroze. He blinked a few times, making sure he was not seeing things. He slowly walked out from behind the tree, and murmured, "How do you know who I am? How come you can talk? Who are you?" He had so many questions.

The owl kept observing Drie, her stare more like a soft gaze at this point. "I am Minerva, I thought you would recognize me."

"How? I have never met you before," Drie said uncomfortably.

"Are you sure?" smiled Minerva, "You may remember my voice, at least."

Drie forced himself to take a deliberate step towards her. He came closer; something about this owl made him feel safe. But he kept a cautious distance and crawled to sit down on the bed of leaves on the forest floor. Now he was eye to eye with the owl.

The gnawing feeling in his gut, the one he often had, returned. He construed that she would know why he kept dreaming of this forest. As though today was the day he would find out about what everything meant; the reason why he felt so hollow and curled up to sleep every night. "Where are we?" Drie asked.

"Hmm, interesting question, Adrian. But is it really important?" Minerva responded, moving a little away from him. No one had called him Adrian in a long time. Lots and lots of questions ran through Drie's mind, as he sat silently on the cold ground, watching her pace around. "A more important question would be, *why* I am here. Or more importantly, *why* you are here…" she stated, and looked at Drie softly.

Drie sat there quietly at a loss of words. Of course, he wanted to know what he was doing here. But he had an inkling that she would not answer. He peered at the owl curiously, waiting for it to say more.

"Do you remember Elie?" Minerva asked, looking at him. Of course, Drie remembered her. She was in his class, and the prettiest girl he knew. Drie used to sit across the classroom from her, and stare at her the entire day, too intimidated to say anything. The light in his eyes was plenty for Minerva to go on.

"Why do you think she left school?" she interrogated.

"I don't know," muttered Drie, confused by this line of questioning. "Are you sure?" asked Minerva. "Do you remember the day you were trying to be cool with your friends, during band practice? You said pretty mean things about her, remember?" she went on. Drie was uncomfortable. How did this owl know all this?

"Yeah, I guess…" responded Drie.

"You said that her family was poor, and she lived on hand-me-downs. Remember?" went on Minerva, pacing up and down the clearing, hobbling lightly on her feet. Drie's gaze followed her all this time.

"I was just fooling around with my friends." Drie replied.

"Of course, you were. But what you did not realise was that, in a matter of days, people started calling her '*hobo.*' This went on for so long that she couldn't take the humiliation, she transferred." Minerva paused in front of Drie, gazed at his eyes and slightly tilted her head.

"Oh. I didn't know," responded Drie, a sudden surge of guilt washing through him.

"Actions have consequences Drie. Always remember that" Minerva stated softly.

"Why are you telling me all this?" Drie asked. "Why are you here, what do you want?" he went on. "Well, the thing is, you have suppressed me for so long, that you cannot hear me anymore. Do you remember the time when you used to pay heed to me? The nagging voice inside your head, telling you when something was wrong? Can you hear me anymore?" She questioned, a feeling of hurt in her eyes.

Drie rubbed his eyes. He could not believe what he was witnessing. What was happening to him? Minerva was right, she had the same voice that Drie heard in his head, but this made no sense to him.

"What are you getting at?" asked Drie. "Are you saying that I have failed you? Disappointed you? What have I done that is so wrong?" asked Drie, exasperated.

"Well, it started small," said Minerva, resuming pacing across the clearing. "Picking up things that do not belong to you, like the school chalks or unattended pens, and then went on to stealing money from the charity box from time to time. You forged your parents' signatures on your test scores and then eventually stated lying at home about school activities and hours. It was all harmless at the beginning, but slowly and steadily you started muffling my voice." Minerva was gazing at the floor while saying all this. She sounded calm, but disappointed. She did not reprimand him, but just narrated incidents off Drie's life in a matter-of-fact manner. "You went on to tease the smart kids of your class with mean anonymous notes and discouraged them from speaking up. You fooled around with the vulnerable, by sliding cards into their lockers. You no longer remained the sweet kid that you were." Minerva looked up, her eyes reflecting the dismay in her voice.

"But you really broke me with what you did last month. Remember your dad gave you money to get a new pair of shoes? He worked so hard to save up that money for you. And you used up that money partying with your friends but told him that someone stole it. You knew that he loved you, you also knew that he would never scold you — you used him." Minerva paused. "You are a good kid, Drie. You shouldn't have done that." She said, with a steady calming gaze.

Before Drie could say anything back, she had disappeared from in front of him. The forest floor slid from under him, and the trees faded away. "Say something, Drie," murmured his aunt in the dining room of his house. "You have to take care of your mother now."

20

Those Green Eyes

by Sindhuja Sarasram

'I'm sorry, you can't deliver your babies inside the house. I'm really sorry, babe, no matter how much you plead... you just can't!' I say, putting up a firm façade, although I am not feeling so sure internally.

She pleads; walking back and forth between me on the front stoop, and the make-shift space I've set up for her. I sold the idea to her a week earlier, but she rated me a poor real-estate agent, and a terrible designer. The latter part hurt me, a licensed architect, the most. Now she checks it out, contemplating. She's torn between accepting *that* and making it inside my house. She cries, and I sigh— revealing my weak resolve.

'I'm sorry, baby!'

From her lime-green irises with hazel specs in them, she stares into my standard-issue dull-brown ones. Fascinating concept, isn't it? Even though, lighter eyes should make one feel comfortable with their transparent nature, one always feels like there's some hidden depth or mystery behind them.

Well, in the moment, I don't think about these fascinating theories because, she comes far too close to my face— her paws land gently on my thighs and touching her nose to mine she seems to drill holes into my brain by gazing eye to eye. Her pupils are narrowing into slits.

This overall gesture doesn't strike me as anger, but the silent intimacy of it all seems to carry a... softness. I am not sure how it happens or what passes between us, but I feel her voice in my head saying *I trust you.* The strangeness of this event gives me goosebumps all over. And it's actually *I trust you** with an asterisk. Now this is the part I interpret for myself, one that goes without saying: **don't you screw this up!*

Oh, and did I not mention that I'm talking about a furball? Sorry! So, here I am— caught in a spell by this very pregnant, very protective, street-smart orange tabby cat— wondering about meaning of the first 30 years of my existence. Her stare has me suddenly feeling confident about having a purpose: parenthood, (even if second-handed.) This purpose, one that I didn't deem to be a part of my future, at least not my immediate future— considering that I am filing for a divorce, living with my parents, stuck in a lost-zone professionally, and not looking for somebody new; after the last time, my ovaries would sooner shrivel than me finding a partner to traverse that territory with.

'Chai, I'm here for you.' I collect her to myself and drop a forehead kiss, brushing her, petting her, and letting her know that I can do this. We can do this. And yes, it was my bright idea to christen her *Chai.* I thought of the endless dad-jokes I could make about chai and milk, but I didn't consider the weird looks I'd receive from folks walking on the street, each time I shout her name. *Have you ever seen a manic teaseller?*

It is 8:00 a.m. on a Thursday and my baby has started labour. This is the occasion that I have been expecting, and dreading, for over 2 months— since the time she lost her then 3-week-old kittens to a male killer-cat, who just wanted to get it on with her. Men will be men, no matter their skin-type.

I am joking about this now, but we all carried— along with considerable guilt— the mother's grief as she'd let strange, wolfish cries of anguish flow into the summer breeze, on the morning of that terrible event. She prowled about those three lifeless, mangled bodies on our roof-top, where she'd been raising them, until midday. The mourning— it took an entire day, some food, a lot of distracting, and offering my lap for her rare acceptance of human comfort, to slowly let them go. The next evening as she kept brushing her cheek against my shoulder, I whispered into her ear, 'I'm sorry, Kiddo. None of us at home saw the danger... until after the incident. I am so sorry.'

Nature is cruel, but there aren't many times I am reminded of the fact. Sure, I know what happens in the wild, or even in other parts of the civilized world— the trials and tribulations people and animals face, thanks to the harshness of the elements. But in my sheltered life, in the very pleasant city of Bangalore, I don't witness them so much. Or maybe, I've got blinders on for so long, and that was the reason for the guilt— for not already anticipating.

***

Chai showed up around the neighbourhood in the November of 2020, as I was looking at the two-and-a-half-year anniversary of my separation from an already estranged marriage— a relationship with clearly no room to hope for a second shot at reviving it. But the taboo of their daughter's divorce loomed over my parents' heads, and I was not ready to measure the strength of their support in standing by my resolve.

Back then, she seemed like a six-months-old kitten; a skinny-little thing that had a nasty, open wound on the side of her torso. She'd sneak under the car, watch and be wary of us humans; even milk, for her hungry stomach, wouldn't entice her. Still feral, she warmed up slowly through the coldness of December, and I made her my new project— despite being subject to cuts, bites and scratches. Some say those are signs of love, the feline way.

***

So here we are at the front stoop, and I tell her, 'You know, I'm really glad you didn't put-out with that stupid, killer-cat.' Chai had a lot of suitors after the death of her first litter, obviously, including the murdering tomcat. 'Still, we could have done without another pregnancy— though, I don't expect *you* to understand planned parenthood. What are we going to do with you?' I sighed.

'Anyway… I'd rather have my ears deal with them— new-borns having scratchy voices like lazy Keto! — than any progeny with psychopathic traits. He was a deadbeat father the first time, and I expect no different now, but that's alright… Us women, together, can raise them on ourselves, can't we?'

'The feminist within me feels good about it. And the rational part of me that understands theory of evolution and how nature works… doesn't know what to say! *Now push!*' I'm taking the role of the midwife-godmother she sanctioned a bit too seriously. I googled, the hell out of, the cat's version of *what to expect when you're expecting.*

A half-hour before, I had to slither my big body under my bed to get to Chai. She had gotten comfortable in a dark corner, behind the tub of laundered clothes that sometimes pleases her, and other household items that see the light once in a blue moon. She's sneaky like that. I think about what kind of a mother I'd be to my future, adopted, human kids. Not a good one apparently, because I can't even teach a cat to behave. *Well, she's a tough cookie to tame!* I console myself.

Chai… must be the human equivalent of a gaslighting person in a relationship, in terms of making one believe that the other's life is incomplete without them. My suspicions might be true considering *Toxoplasmosis*, which I'm sure she's infected me with. I do sometimes think— *I need her in my life, and I am not doing enough.* As a family, we had been dog-people all these years and here comes this cat, thrusting this memo at my face: *You're a cat lady. You better start believing it.*

So, I sit there in front of the entrance door with this vagabond on my lap— another rare occurrence which she initiates herself. Her purring is continuous and part of me vibrates along with her. I hear it is a privilege if a cat trusts you so much as to give birth around you, but all I can currently sense is that she's afraid. 'Baby, come on! You can do this! You're going to give birth to beautiful babies, and we are going to take great care of them. I promise! I am going to hold your hand through it all… I mean, your paw- whichever noun you prefer.' I don't know how many kittens she has inside of her, because unlike the last time— when we didn't even realise that she was carrying— she now looks like a large papaya, held up on sticks.

***

It has been an hour since we sat down. I think, *is this a normal labour?* I wonder how Chai managed it all by herself the last time— sneaking up on our terrace, going through it alone until my mother found her and the little ones, in one of the empty plant pots. Several googles later, I know that there have been rare occurrences of difficult cat-labour and it can take anything between 4-16 hours for the entire affair. And I feel wetness on my thigh as her water breaks. *Hallelujah!*

As the first kitten comes, she makes her way into the litter box I've set up for the purpose- it includes a deep, plastic, vegetable-crate for a base; a taped-up cardboard roof made twice as tall as the bottom; and an old, cotton vest making for a comfortable floor. Not a creation I can proudly add to my portfolio of works, but it will do. Out plonks a dark-pink creature out of her, amidst a lot of goo. And this is the first time I am witnessing childbirth, and it comes as a surprise to me that I haven't thrown up yet. *Me:1: Tokophobia:0.*

It's 12:00 p.m. now, and she's surrounded by five, cute-little beings she gave birth to— over the last 3 hours. I think her womb is done releasing all ejective matter. As she licks the young-ones clean, and their fur dries, they start appearing like frizzy balls of orange. It is so captivating, how their mouths find their way over to her nipples, to get fed. They move like blind fish, navigating by way of touch as their eyes aren't open yet. I gently finger one of the paws, nude, tender and pink, poking out through the holes of the basket. And I know I'm in love. And maybe… that is why, late in the evening I commit— the first-ever decision I've taken, about someone apart from myself— to bring them into the house, after all. I want to protect this bunch— keep them safe and indoors for 8-9 weeks— until they can be weaned away from their mother and adopted. 'Alright Chai, I'm going to take care of you all! Let's go inside now!'

***

In the first few days, Chai leaves me to honour my matronly duties whenever she's done feeding her litter. She leaps through a bathroom window, and onto my neighbour's roof— because the mostly-vegetarian diet I feed her is too basic, and because she likes her freedom. She spends her time, outdoors, looking for rats; or when she's feeling spicy or exotic, the victim is a squirrel or a small bird. I haven't stopped her from doing so, even now, as long as all of her gastronomical needs are taken care outside the house. Being a vagabond and never a jailbird, she's always been free to roam and feed on whatever she wants— I know I can't suddenly change all that.

Two weeks down, the kittens have opened their eyes, their ears move, they can smell, and they are teething. And I often sit with them, admiring their sleeping faces and making a list of names for the kittens. Having learnt about conceptualising and all that jazz, in grad school— I come up with theme-based sets of names. One can never get too serious about those. There's one with tea-time snacks; there's one with varieties of the fruit orange; shades of the colour orange; another with an autumn-theme; and then there's everybody's favourite— based on types of tea drinks— Lemon, Basil, Bubble, Masala and Ginger.

I identify a kitten by a patch of dark fur on the back of its head, and another, which is not as textured as the other siblings— that one's a screamer to boot; each of their unique characteristics are unravelling and I don't think any of my themes justify their individual nature. So, I throw my lists into the garbage. Three weeks old now, they're all curious about corners; they are springy, energetic, and light-footed. They also start pooping, and while cleaning up the mess— I have a revelation, 'Umm... Chai, have you been eating their poop all along? I, *Eww*… I don't even know what to say!' I try to count the number of times I've peppered her face with kisses.

At four weeks, they start eating solid food and get comfortable with the idea of human presence— they start burrowing themselves into my lap; sometimes Chai joins them and cuddles in my warmth. By now I've started taking their pictures like professional photographers do with baby-photoshoots and uploading on social media— with hopes that there are people out there, who'd want to shelter these innocent souls.

***

'No. NO. You cannot bring that inside. I'm sorry,' I assert. It's week six, and the mother cat stands at my door with a rat in her mouth. Still, over the next week, she brings a dead animal whenever she can manage. I realise she wants to feed the rodents to her young ones— but I don't allow her to. My family says I should probably let her march the kittens out, and that I'm interfering with their natural growth.

Her escapade through the window is more frequent now than ever before, and she's restless to stay indoors. When I let her outside, she wants me to let the kittens follow her. And since I don't allow that, she sits outside my workspace and meows away her disappointment in me. I think Chai still cares for me despite my rules, but I wonder if she sees me as dictatorial.

While working, in my space, I hear one of the kittens screaming. I walk into the bathroom, to the scene of Chai daring to jump over to the neighbour's terrace with a kitty in her mouth; there was another incident where she unsuccessfully tried to push another little puss through the kitchen ventilator's grill.

I stop her attempt— but through her mad eyes, I finally understand the desperation of the mother. 'What are you doing? — You're going to kill them!' I take a breather, before continuing. 'Now listen up, kid. I will not have any of this. They are going to stay indoors until they are old enough to be adopted. And they have to eat whatever the people in their new homes provide for them. Don't ruin their future!' Only after the words are out of my mouth, I realise the hypocrisy of my behaviour. I have forever been dismayed by this society that raises girls to be empty shells, ones that get formed fully only when married and sent to 'live' at their in-laws. I draw a weird kind of parallel between the two situations, and it is unsettling to say the least.

Soon I'm having a meltdown about the only second decision I'm making about lives other than mine— I thought I could do this; help raise these kittens in a protected environment and give them away to people interested in adopting. But currently, it is freaking me out. I wonder if I should have my therapist pick my brain again. I comb my short hair with my fingers, and outcome a few strands of hair, with every stroke. I binge through half a day's worth of comedy-drama series. It's the late afternoon, by the time I pull myself together.

So, there we are, Chai and I sitting on the floor. 'I know, you didn't trade your freedom, or theirs, for the safety of staying indoors. I can't believe I got so caught up with doing what's right and what I can control, that I stopped considering your feelings. You're a good kid— for forgiving me. You do, right? Forgive me?'

I look at her. 'You know, Chai, it's kinda insulting that I go about giving you these big, elaborate monologues, and you, you are so… withholding!'

She gives me this languid fluttering blink and I know we are alright. Sunrays filter through my window, some of them causing her jade-like irises to glint. Suddenly, I'm transported to another time and place.

It was a few months ago, when I was sitting on the rocky embankments of the bay-of-Bengal in French town, Pondicherry. It was a little after the first light. I was thinking about the hand I had been dealt— so far, not much of goodness had come out of it and wondering when I was going to get my break and when I can start commanding the direction my life is heading towards, while also feeling old— about reaching my 30s with no significant accomplishments. But looking at the sky, my eyes caught the green flash just before the sun showed itself. It had felt like the universe had responded to my thoughts. It seemed a lot like hope.

For so long, I've lived my life being a supporting character— not realising that it is my story and I'm the protagonist. It took this tiny soul, all of 8 pounds- to remind myself of it.

The next morning, I call her upstairs and let her take the kittens with her… wherever. I don't know for sure if they'll be around me as they grow up, if they'll get adopted, or if they'll all make it. And

I don't know what I am going to do with the rest of my life. But Chai has definitely taught me to finally be the main character of my life, and I think her will to survive is rubbing off on me. We take care of our own and put our own damn selves first. I hope, and I think, we'll be alright.

Meet the strangers
who made this book

P.R.M.

P.R.M. is Priyamvada, Pri, Priya, Divya and the best of all, Vada (depending on who you ask.) She's someone who's always looking for inspiration in the daily mundane. She's 50% homesick, 30% foodie, 15% HANGRY and 5% your usual girl-next-door. She grew up primarily in Bangalore, but has a bit of Punekar still left in her. She found her love and passion in Art and Architecture. Navigating life and work in Denver, her latest challenge is creating a balance.

Halo Golwin

Halo Golwin is not merely a symbol, but an epithet for Golwin's whimsical friend who inspired him to exercise personal freedom through writing. With the might of the pen, Halo Golwin's works often bring out the absurd in the mundane, and utilise humour to amplify the insane. If you are an avid lover of poetry and art, do visit @not_a_blank_slate_anymore on Instagram!

Suchitra Moorty

Suchitra Moorty is a management professional residing in New Delhi, India. She has spent 18 years working across industries, profiles, and countries. Of late, she has realised that her true calling is writing and is all set to make a quest for it. A Grammar-Nazi, a poetess and a wannabe authoress is who Suchitra is.

Isha Sharma

To see a twist in the mundane, the fantastic in ordinary and the poetic in our chaotic world is what Isha aspires to achieve in her work. With a degree in English literature, a diploma in film studies and a decade long experience in entertainment production, she currently freelances as a writer and media consultant. She is also finishing her first novel.

One can find her on Instagram @ishasharma_22 and Twitter @ishasharma2282.

Raghavi Shankara Guhan

Raghavi is a humble and cheerful soul, currently pursuing her Diploma in Biotechnology. She loves to engage in performing arts — dance and music are her hobbies. She is also a reading-addict, from which her interest in writing stemmed. Her poems and stories are ingrained with a profound sense of morals and values; she often tries to layer her work, creating subtleties.

Eden Cardoz

Eden Cardoz is a 19-year-old college-goer. Born in Dubai and brought up in Mumbai. She loves to write her heart out, expressing her life and thoughts through her words. It is what she does best. She lives for the adventures of exploring new chapters in her life. You can find her on Instagram @eden_cardoz.

Shibani Sharma

Shibani Sharma is a millennial writer with a full-time job in admissions, at an international school. An alumnus of the Mithibai College, Mumbai, she is passionate about the literary world; reading and writing are her best friends. She is optimistic, and believes in nurturing relationships, highly valuing emotional intelligence. Apart from her husband and family, you can always find her around pets. *The six sparks* is her first published story, with more in the pipeline. Her Instagram handle is @shibani.sharma.919

Shalini Ray

Shalini Ray is a twenty-three-year-old scriptwriter and filmmaker. She was born in Kolkata, now shuffles between Mumbai and Delhi. She likes to write metafiction, magical realism, and everything in the middle. Her subjects are usually women and their everyday lives. She tells stories through visuals on Instagram at @shaliniiray.

Jigyasa Tandon

Jigyasa Tandon is a trained Mental health Educationist at NIMHANS, Bangalore, where she practices as a Counselling Psychologist. She is also a teacher and author. She was a part of the poetry collection, Echoes of a Rebellious Mind. You can connect with her on Instagram @jigyasasaysthisway.

Aanika Gajendragad

Aanika Gajendragad is a promising 14-year-old. She is being home-schooled to focus on writing, rather than the subjects that never interested her — Math and Science. She's been passionate about writing since the age of 9, and making a career out of it seemed like the natural choice. She has a website for short stories where she also blogs: muchbyaanika.com. You can also follow her on Instagram, Facebook, and Twitter @muchbyaanika.

Kongkona Baishya

Kongkona Baishya is a teacher from Assam, with a post-graduation in English Literature. An amateur, she writes stories and poems in local platforms. She has also completed her internship in Acting from TD Film Studio, Guwahati, and is currently pursuing her passion as an actress.

Prerna Singh

Prerna Singh is a dreamer by the day, lawyer by the night and a writer somewhere in between. A fitness enthusiast, she likes to try different forms of workout. She operates in extremes and is not sure what she enjoys more—activity or inactivity. She aspires to be a serial traveller and a full-time writer someday (ideally housed at a cosy cottage amidst the hills.) For her take on life and travel, follow her on Instagram @prernasingh08 and https://livelovewandercreate.blogspot.com/

Yumna Usmani

Yumna Usmani is a teen who lives with her big-fat-joint family in Bhopal, and is mostly found lying on the couch, reading. She has a penchant for public-speaking, baking, and writing. She enjoys spouting off sarcastic remarks with her cousins. Reruns of *friends* are the major staple on bad days. 24/7 flow of chai can be found in her veins.

Yash Karmancherry

Yash Karmancherry is a traveller, outdoor enthusiast, and friend of earth. Just a 20-something-old who believes he can make a change with his individual actions. Growing up in the concrete jungles of Mumbai, he was intrigued to explore if the grass was literally greener on the other side, and he realises that IT IS!

Sharad Narayan

Sharad Narayan has a diverse range of interests, of which writing is one. He is an amateur naturalist, frequently visiting biodiversity hotspots for walks and photography. He plays the veena, and is a part of a group of performers called Sapthasakhi. He is a practicing architect and currently a faculty at a noted college for architecture in Bangalore.

James Bowers

James Bowers loves to write; he loves writing so much that it keeps him sane. You can read more of his work on Instagram @writing_to_stay_sane.

Whether he's making money out of it or not isn't really his concern; all he wants is for someone to read what he has written and connect with it.

Pritha Samanta

Some believe in God, some in the Universe. Pritha believes in stories and dreams. An architect by profession, she likes to conjure situations and settings for a full-time job. When not working, she finds ways to satisfy her wanderlust or create some lip-smacking dishes. She is particular about things and loves to narrate. Through her stories, Pritha wishes to create a sense of empathy and belonging.

Sree Yelamanchi

Sree Yelamanchi is a doctor by profession and a writer by passion. She chose writing to get through the dark days of her life, eventually fell in love with it, and now believes: *It's the pen that chooses you.* Books, coffee, and chocolate are her happy place. She plans to live the rest of her life taking it as and how it comes, just one day at a time.

Acknowledgements

Thank you, dear reader, for picking up this book.

Aparnaa and Priyamvada — my go-to beta readers and my soul sisters — please take a bow!

Pritha, when I look back, my writing journey started when I met you; So, thank you for inspiring, for the honour of letting me make suggestions during those tss days, and for the promise of editing your future work (I'm waiting on it, no pressure.)

For Inkfeathers Publishing team, especially the Editors' & Publishing Managers, Tanishk (I was very tempted to add a Q here, and you know it!) and Uma, for all the handholding. I thank everyone else involved, and editorial board — from the bottom of my heart, for this publishing set-up that has made it easy for writers like me to even make an attempt such as this. Thank you for putting me one step closer to the dream.

For my writers, I feel insurmountable gratitude for trusting your works with me, and for your patience and support through the entire duration of this baby's delivery.

To the master storytellers who don't know of my existence— Taylor Swift, Malcolm Gladwell, Billie Joe Armstrong, Christopher Nolan and Bjarke Ingels. And the essayists of the Modern Love column. And the writers of This Is Us. (Okay, I'll stop now.) I am grateful they exist and influence me.

To friends who've cheered me on. To my therapist, who's helping me bring about the real me. For those English teachers who taught me well enough that I felt like I could call at least one language as mine. And finally, my family, for the little encouragements made, to read — it's making a full circle.

You can listen to the
'Everybody's A Stranger' inspired playlist
put together by our authors here:

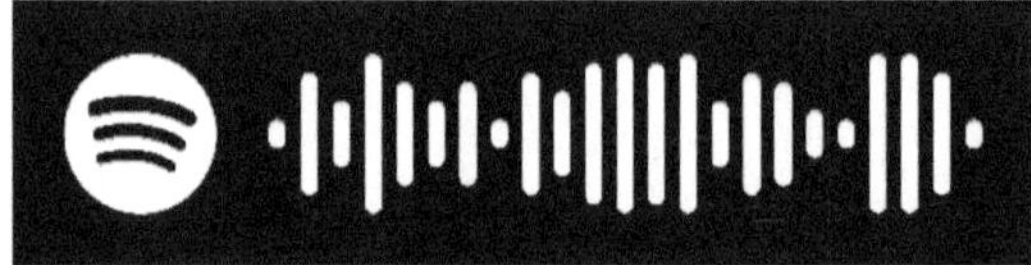

INKFEATHERS PUBLISHING

India's Most Author Friendly Publishing House

Stay updated about the latest books, anthologies, events, exclusive offers, contests, product giveaways and other things that we do to support authors.

 Inkfeathers Publishing

 @InkfeathersPublishing

 @_Inkfeathers

 @Inkfeathers

 Inkfeathers.com

We'd love to connect with you!

www.ingramcontent.com/pod-product-compliance
Lightning Source LLC
LaVergne TN
LVHW091206150826
845672LV00005B/1259

* 9 7 8 9 3 9 0 8 8 2 5 4 0 *